The Man of the Desert

She gave a quick frightened glance around and then her eyes besought him. All the terror of the night alone returned upon her. She heard again the howl of the coyotes, and saw the long dark shadows of the canyon.

"Oh, don't leave me alone!" Hazel said.

There was that in her appealing helplessness that gave him a wild desire to stoop and fold her in his arms. The color came and went in his fine bronzed face, and his eyes grew tender with feeling.

"I won't leave you," the missionary said. Only God knew what was passing in his soul—a great longing to have her always near him, to ever protect her from the storms of life.

Bantam Books by Grace Livingston Hill
Ask your bookseller for the books you have missed

The Man of the Desert

Grace Livingston Hill

BANTAM BOOKS
TORONTO · NEW YORK · LONDON · SYDNEY

THE MAN OF THE DESERT

*A Bantam Book / published by arrangement with
Harper & Row, Publishers Inc.*

Bantam edition / February 1982

ISBN 0-553-20286-3

Published simultaneously in the United States and Canada

Bantam Books are published by Bantam Books, Inc. Its trademark,
consisting of the words ''Bantam Books'' and the portrayal of a
rooster, is Registered in U.S. Patent and Trademark Office and in
other countries. Marca Registrada. Bantam Books, Inc., 666 Fifth
Avenue, New York, New York 10103.

PRINTED IN THE UNITED STATES OF AMERICA

0 9 8 7 6 5 4 3 2 1

Contents

·I·

Prospecting

It was morning, high and clear as Arizona counts weather, and around the little railroad station were gathered a crowd of curious onlookers; seven Indians, three women from near-by shacks—drawn thither by the sight of the great private car that the night express had left on a side track—the usual number of loungers, a swarm of children, besides the station agent who had come out to watch proceedings.

All the morning the private car had been an object of deep interest to those who lived within sight, and that was everybody on the plateau; and many and various had been the errands and excuses to go to the station that perchance the occupants of that car might be seen, or a glimpse of the interior of the moving palace; but the silken curtains had remained drawn until after nine o'clock.

Within the last half hour, however, a change had taken place in the silent inscrutable car. The curtains had parted here and there, revealing dim flitting faces, a table spread with a snowy cloth and flowers in a vase, wild flowers they were, too, like those that grew all along the track, just weeds. Strange that one who could afford a private car cared for weeds in a glass on their dining table, but then perhaps they didn't know.

A fat cook with ebony skin and white linen attire had appeared on the rear platform beating eggs, and half whistling, half singing:

> "Be my little baby Bumble-bee—
> Buzz around, buzz around—"

He seemed in no wise affected or embarrassed by the natives who gradually encircled the end of the car, and the audience grew.

They could dimly see the table where the inmates of the car were—dining?—it couldn't be breakfast at that hour surely. They heard the discussion about horses going on amid laughter and merry conversation, and they gathered that the car was to remain here for the day at least while some of the party went off on a horseback trip. It was nothing very unusual of course. Such things occasionally occurred in that region, but not often enough to lose their interest. Besides, to watch the tourists who chanced to stop in their tiny settlement was the only way for them to learn the fashions.

Not that all the watchers stood and stared around the car. No, indeed. They made their headquarters around the station platform from whence they took brief and comprehensive excursions down to the freight station and back, going always on one side of the car and returning by way of the other. Even the station agent felt the importance of the occasion, and stood around with all the self-consciousness of an usher at a grand wedding, considering himself master of ceremonies.

"Sure! They come from the East last night. Limited dropped 'em! Going down to prospect some mine, I reckon. They ordered horses an' a outfit, and Shag Bunce is goin' with 'em. He got a letter 'bout a week ago tellin' what they wanted of him. Yes, I knowed all about it. He brung the letter to me to cipher out fer him. You know Shag ain't no great at readin' ef he is the best judge of a mine anywheres about."

Thus the station agent explained in low thrilling tones; and even the Indians watched and grunted their interest.

At eleven o'clock the horses arrived, four besides Shag's, and the rest of the outfit. The onlookers regarded Shag with the mournful interest due to the undertaker at a funeral. Shag felt it and acted accordingly. He gave short, gruff orders to his men: called attention to straps and buckles that every one knew were in as perfect order as they could be; criticized the horses and his men; and every one, even the horses, bore it with perfect composure. They were all showing off and felt the importance of the moment.

Presently the car door opened and Mr. Radcliffe came out on the platform and accompanied by his son—a handsome reckless looking fellow—his daughter Hazel, and Mr. Hamar, a thick-set, heavy-featured man with dark hair, jaunty black

2

moustache and handsome black eyes. In the background stood an erect elderly woman in tailor-made attire and with a severe expression, Mr. Radcliffe's elder sister who was taking the trip with them expecting to remain in California with her son; and behind her hovered Hazel's maid. These two were not to be of the riding party, it appeared.

There was a pleasant stir while the horses were brought forward and the riders were mounting. The spectators remained breathlessly unconscious of anything save the scene being enacted before them. Their eyes lingered with special interest on the girl of the party.

Miss Radcliffe was small and graceful, with a head set on her pretty shoulders like a flower on its stem. Moreover she was fair, so fair that she almost dazzled the eyes of the men and women accustomed to brown cheeks kissed by the sun and wind of the plain. There was a wild-rose pink in her cheeks to enhance the whiteness, which made it but the more dazzling. She had masses of golden hair wreathed round her dainty head in a bewilderment of waves and braids. She had great dark eyes of blue set off by long curling lashes, and delicately pencilled dark brows which gave the eyes a pansy softness and made you feel when she looked at you that she meant a great deal more by the look than you had at first suspected. They were wonderful, beautiful eyes, and the little company of idlers at the station were promptly bewitched by them. Moreover there was a fantastic little dimple in her right cheek that flashed into view at the same time with the gleam of pearly teeth when she smiled. She certainly was a picture. The station looked its fill and rejoiced in her young beauty.

She was garbed in a dark green riding habit, the same that she wore when she rode attended by her groom in Central Park. It made a sensation among the onlookers, as did the little riding cap of dark green velvet and the pretty riding gloves. She sat her pony well, daintily, as though she had alighted briefly, but to their eyes strangely, and not as the women out there rode. On the whole the station saw little else but the girl; all the others were mere accessories to the picture.

They noticed indeed that the young man, whose close cropped golden curls, and dark lashed blue eyes were so like the girl's that he could be none other than her brother, rode

3

beside the older man who was presumably the father; and that the dark, handsome stranger rode away beside the girl. Not a man of them but resented it. Not a woman of them but regretted it.

Then Shag Bunce, with a parting word to his small but complete outfit that rode behind, put spurs to his horse, lifted his sombrero in homage to the lady, and shot to the front of the line, his shaggy mane by which came his name floating over his shoulders. Out into the sunshine of a perfect day the riders went, and the group around the platform stood silently and watched until they were a speck in the distance blurring with the sunny plain and occasional ash and cottonwood trees.

"I seen the missionary go by early this mornin'," speculated the station agent meditatively, deliberately, as though he only had a right to break the silence. "I wonder whar he could 'a' bin goin'. He passed on t'other side the track er I'd 'a' ast 'im. He 'peared in a turrible hurry. Anybody sick over towards the canyon way?"

"Buck's papoose heap sick!" muttered an immobile Indian, and shuffled off the platform with a stolid face. The women heaved a sigh of disappointment and turned to go. The show was out and they must return to the monotony of their lives. They wondered what it would be like to ride off like that into the sunshine with cheeks like roses and eyes that saw nothing but pleasure ahead. What would a life like that be? Awed, speculative, they went back to their sturdy children and their ill-kept houses, to sit in the sun on the doorsteps and muse a while.

Into the sunshine rode Hazel Radcliffe well content with the world, herself, and her escort.

Milton Hamar was good company. He was keen of wit and a past-master in the delicate art of flattery. That he was fabulously wealthy and popular in New York society; that he was her father's friend both socially and financially, and had been much of late in their home on account of some vast mining enterprise in which both were interested; and that his wife was said to be uncongenial and always interested in other men rather than her husband, were all facts that combined to give Hazel a pleasant, half-romantic interest in the man by her side. She had been conscious of a sense of

4

satisfaction and pleasant anticipation when her father told her that he was to be of their party. His wit and gallantry would make up for the necessity of having her Aunt Maria along. Aunt Maria was always a damper to anything she came near. She was the personification of propriety. She had tried to make Hazel think she must remain in the car and rest that day instead of going off on a wild goose chase after a mine. No lady did such things, she told her niece.

Hazel's laugh rang out like the notes of a bird as the two rode slowly down the trail, not hurrying, for there was plenty of time. They could meet the others on their way back if they did not get to the mine so soon, and the morning was lovely.

Milton Hamar could appreciate the beauties of nature now and then. He called attention to the line of hills in the distance, and the sharp steep peak of a mountain piercing the sunlight. Then skillfully he led his speech around to his companion, and showed how lovelier than the morning she was.

He had been indulging in such delicate flattery since they first started from New York, whenever the indefatigable aunt left them alone long enough, but this morning there was a note of something closer and more intimate in his words; a warmth of tenderness that implied unspeakable joy in her beauty, such as he had never dared to use before. It flattered her pride deliciously. It was beautiful to be young and charming and have a man say such things with a look like that in his eyes—eyes that had suffered, and appealed to her to pity. With her young, innocent heart she did pity, and was glad she might solace his sadness a little while.

With consummate skill the man led her to talk of himself, his hopes in youth, his disappointments, his bitter sadness, his heart loneliness. He suddenly asked her to call him Milton, and the girl with rosy cheeks and dewy eyes declared shyly that she never could, it would seem so queer, but she finally compromised after much urging on "Cousin Milton."

"That will do for a while," he succumbed, smiling as he looked at her with impatient eyes. Then with growing intimacy in his tones he laid a detaining hand upon hers that held the bridle, and the horses both slackened their gait, though they had been far behind the rest of the party for over an hour now.

"Listen, little girl," he said, "I'm going to open my heart to you. I'm going to tell you a secret."

Hazel sat very still, half alarmed at his tone, not daring to withdraw her hand, for she felt the occasion was momentous and she must be ready with her sympathy as any true friend would be. Her heart swelled with pride that it was to her he came in his trouble. Then she looked up into the face that was bending over hers, and she saw triumph, not trouble, in his eyes. Even then she did not understand.

"What is it?" she asked trustingly.

"Dear child!" said the man of the world impressively, "I knew you would be interested. Well, I will tell you. I have told you of my sorrow, now I will tell you of my joy. It is this: When I return to New York I shall be a free man. Everything is complete at last. I have been granted a divorce from Ellen, and there remain only a few technicalities to be attended to. Then we shall be free to go our ways and do as we choose."

"A divorce!" gasped Hazel appalled. "Not you—divorced!"

"Yes," affirmed the happy man gaily, "I knew you'd be surprised. It's almost too good to be true, isn't it, after all my trouble to get Ellen to consent?"

"But she—your wife—where will she go? What will she do?" Hazel looked up at him with troubled eyes, half bewildered with the thought.

She did not realize that the horses had stopped and that he still held her hand which grasped the bridle.

"Oh, Ellen will be married at once," he answered flippantly. "That's the reason she's consented at last. She's going to marry Walling Stacy, you know, and from being stubborn about it, she's quite in a hurry to make any arrangement to fix things up now."

"She's going to be married!" gasped Hazel as if she had not heard of such things often. Somehow it had never come quite so close to her list of friendships before and it shocked her inexpressibly.

"Yes, she's going to be married at once, so you see there's no need to think of her ever again. But why don't you ask me what I am going to do?"

"Oh, yes!" said Hazel recalling her lack of sympathy at once. "You startled me so. What are you going to do? You

6

poor man—what can you do? Oh, I am so sorry for you!" and the pansy-eyes became suffused with tears.

"No need to feel sorry for me, little one," said the exultant voice, and he looked at her now with an expression she had never seen in his face before. "I shall be happy as I have never dreamed of before," he said. "I am going to be married too. I am going to marry some one who loves me with all her heart, and I am sure of that, though she has never told me so. I am going to marry you, little sweetheart!" He stooped suddenly before she could take in the meaning of his words, and flinging his free arm about her pressed his lips upon hers.

With a wild cry like some terrified creature Hazel tried to draw herself away, and finding herself held fast her quick anger rose and she lifted the hand which held the whip and blindly slashed the air about her; her eyes closed, her heart swelling with horror and fear. A great repulsion for the man whom hitherto she had regarded with deep respect surged over her. To get away from him at once was her greatest desire. She lashed out again with her whip, blindly, not seeing what she struck, almost beside herself with wrath and fear.

Hamar's horse reared and plunged, almost unseating his rider, and as he struggled to keep his seat, having necessarily released the girl from his embrace, the second cut of the whip took him stingingly across the eyes, causing him to cry out with the pain. The horse reared again and sent him sprawling upon the ground, his hands to his face, his senses one blank of pain for the moment.

Hazel, knowing only that she was free, followed an instinct of fear and struck her own pony on the flank, causing the little beast to turn sharply to right angles with the trail he had been following and dart like a streak across the level plateau. Thereafter the girl had all she could do to keep her seat.

She had been wont to enjoy a run in the Park with her groom at safe distance behind her. She was proud of her ability to ride, and could take fences as well as her young brother; but a run like this across an illimitable space, on a creature of speed like the wind, goaded by fear and knowing the limitations of his rider, was a different matter. The swift flight took her breath away, and unnerved her. She tried to

7

hold on to the saddle with her shaking hands, for the bridle was already flying loose to the breeze, but her hold seemed so slight that each moment she expected to find herself lying huddled on the plain with the pony far in the distance.

Her lips grew white and cold; her breath came short and painfully; her eyes were strained with trying to look ahead at the constantly receding horizon. Was there no end? Would they never come to a human habitation? Would no one ever come to her rescue? How long could a pony stand a pace like this? And how long could she hope to hold on to the furious flying creature?

Off to the right at last she thought she saw a building. It seemed hours they had been flying through space. In a second they were close by it. It was a cabin, standing alone upon the great plain with sage-brush in patches about the door and a neat rail fence around it.

She could see one window at the end, and a tiny chimney at the back. Could it be that any one lived in such a forlorn spot?

Summoning all her strength as they neared the spot she flung her voice out in a wild appeal while the pony hurled on, but the wind caught the feeble effort and flung it away into the vast spaces like a little torn worthless fragment of sound.

Tears stung their way into her wide dry eyes. The last hairpin left its mooring and slipped down to earth. The loosened golden hair streamed back on the wind like hands of despair wildly clutching for help, and the jaunty green riding cap was snatched by the breeze and hung upon a sage-bush not fifty feet from the cabin gate, but the pony rushed on with the frightened girl still clinging to the saddle.

II

The Man

About noon of the same day the missionary halted his horse on the edge of a great flat-topped mesa and looked away to the clear blue mountains in the distance.

John Brownleigh had been in Arizona for nearly three years, yet the wonder of the desert had not ceased to charm him, and now as he stopped his horse to rest, his eyes sought the vast distances stretched in every direction, and revelled in the splendour of the scene.

Those mountains at which he was gazing were more than a hundred miles from him, and yet they stood out clear and distinct in the wonderful air, and seemed but a short journey away.

Below him were ledges of rock in marvellous colours, yellow and gray, crimson and green piled one upon another, with the strange light of the noonday sun playing over them and turning their colours into a blaze of glory. Beyond was a stretch of sand, broken here and there by sage-brush, grease-wood, or cactus rearing its prickly spines grotesquely.

Off to the left were pink tinted cliffs and a little farther dark cone-like buttes. On the other hand low brown and white hills stretched away to the wonderful petrified forest, where great tracts of fallen tree trunks and chips lay locked in glistening stone.

To the south he could see the familiar water-hole, and farther the entrance to the canyon, fringed with cedars and pines. The grandeur of the scene impressed him anew.

"Beautiful, beautiful!" he murmured, "and a grand God to have it so!" Then a shadow of sadness passed over his face, and he spoke again aloud as had come to be his habit in this vast loneliness.

"I guess it is worth it," he said, "worth all the lonely days

9

and discouraging months and disappointments, just to be alone with a wonderful Father like mine!''

He had just come from a three days' trip in company with another missionary whose station was a two days' journey by horseback from his own, and whose cheery little home was presided over by a sweet-faced woman, come recently from the East to share his fortunes. The delicious dinner prepared for her husband and his guests, the air of comfort in the three-roomed shack, the dainty touches that showed a woman's hand, had filled Brownleigh with a noble envy. Not until this visit had he realized how very much alone his life was.

He was busy of course from morning till night, and his enthusiasm for his work was even greater than when nearly three years before he had been sent out by the Board to minister to the needs of the Indians. Friends he had by the score. Wherever a white man or trader lived in the region he was always welcome; and the Indians knew and loved his coming. He had come around this way now to visit an Indian hogan where the shadow of death was hovering over a little Indian maiden beloved of her father. It had been a long way around and the missionary was weary with many days in the saddle, but he was glad he had come. The little maid had smiled to see him, and felt that the dark valley of death seemed more to her now like one of her own flower-lit canyons that led out to a brighter, wider day, since she had heard the message of life he brought her.

But as he looked afar over the long way he had come, and thought of the bright little home where he had dined the day before, the sadness still lingered in his face.

''It would be good to have somebody like that,'' he said, aloud again, ''somebody to expect me, and be glad,—but then''—thoughtfully—''I suppose there are not many girls who are willing to give up their homes and go out to rough it as she has done. It is a hard life for a woman—for that kind of a woman!'' A pause, then, ''And I wouldn't want any other kind!''

His eyes grew large with wistfulness. It was not often thus that the cheery missionary stopped to think upon his own lot in life. His heart was in his work, and he could turn his hand to anything. There was always plenty to be done. Yet to-day for some inexplicable reason, for the first time since he had

10

really got into the work and outgrown his first homesickness, he was hungry for companionship. He had seen a light in the eyes of his fellow-missionary that spoke eloquently of the comfort and joy he himself had missed and it struck deep into his heart. He had stopped here on this mesa, with the vast panorama of the desert spread before him, to have it out with himself.

The horse breathed restfully, drooping his head and closing his eyes to make the most of the brief respite, and the man sat thinking, trying to fill his soul with the beauty of the scene and crowd out the longings that had pressed upon him. Suddenly he raised his head with a quiet upward motion and said reverently:

"Oh, my Christ, you knew what this loneliness was! You were lonely too! It is the way you went, and I will walk with you! That will be good."

He sat for a moment with uplifted face towards the vast sky, his fine strong features touched with a tender light, their sadness changing into peace. Then with the old cheery brightness coming into his face again he returned to the earth and its duties.

"Billy, it's time we were getting on," he remarked to his horse chummily. "Do you see that sun in the heavens? It'll get there before we do if we don't look out, and we're due at the fort to-night if we can possibly make it. We had too much vacation, that's about the size of it, and we're spoiled! We're lazy, Billy! We'll have to get down to work. Now how about it? Can we get to that water-hole in half an hour? Let's try for it, old fellow, and then we'll have a good drink, and a bite to eat, and maybe ten minutes for a nap before we take the short trail home. There's some of the corn chop left for you, Billy, so hustle up, old boy, and get there."

Billy, with an answering snort, responded to his master's words, and carefully picked his way over boulders and rocks down to the valley below.

But within a half mile of the water-hole the young man suddenly halted his horse and sprang from the saddle, stooping in the sand beside a tall yucca to pick up something that gleamed like fire in the sunlight. In all that brilliant glowing landscape a bit of brightness had caught his eye and insistently flung itself upon his notice as worthy of investigation.

11

There was something about the sharp light it flung that spoke of another world than the desert. John Brownleigh could not pass it by. It might be only a bit of broken glass from an empty flask flung carelessly aside, but it did not look like that. He must see.

Wondering he stooped and picked it up, a bit of bright gold on the handle of a handsome riding whip. It was not such a whip as people in this region carried; it was dainty, costly, elegant, a lady's riding whip! It spoke of a world of wealth and attention to expensive details, as far removed from this scene as possible. Brownleigh stood still in wonder and turned the pretty trinket over in his hand. Now how did that whip come to be lying in a bunch of sage-brush on the desert? Jewelled, too, and that must have given the final keen point of light to the flame which made him stop short in the sand to pick it up. It was a single clear stone of transparent yellow, a topaz likely, he thought, but wonderfully alive with light, set in the end of the handle, and looking closely he saw a handsome monogram engraved on the side, and made out the letters H. R. But that told him nothing.

With knit brows he pondered, one foot in the stirrup, the other still upon the desert, looking at the elegant toy. Now who, *who* would be so foolish as to bring a thing like that into the desert? There were no lady riders anywhere about that he knew, save the major's sister at the military station, and she was most plain in all her appointments. This frivolous implement of horsemanship never belonged to the major's sister. Tourists seldom came this way. What did it mean?

He sprang into the saddle and shading his eyes with his hand scanned the plain, but only the warm shimmer of sun-heated earth appeared. Nothing living could be seen. What ought he to do about it? Was there any way he might find out the owner and restore the lost property?

Pondering thus, his eyes divided between the distance and the glittering whip-handle, they came to the water-hole; and Brownleigh dismounted, his thoughts still upon the little whip.

"It's very strange, Billy. I can't make out a theory that suits me," he mused aloud. "If any one has been riding out this way and lost it, will they perhaps return and look for it? Yet if I leave it where I found it the sand might drift over it at any time. And surely, in this sparsely settled country, I shall be able to at least hear of any strangers who might have carried such a foolish little thing. Then, too, if I leave it where I found it some one might steal it. Well, I guess we'll take it with us, Billy; we'll hear of the owner somewhere some time no doubt."

The horse answered with a snort of satisfaction as he lifted his moist muzzle from the edge of the water and looked contentedly about.

The missionary unstrapped his saddle and flung it on the ground, unfastening the bag of "corn chop" and spreading it conveniently before his dumb companion. Then he set about gathering a few sticks from near at hand and started a little blaze. In a few minutes the water was bubbling cheerfully in his little folding tin cup for a cup of tea, and a bit of bacon was frying in a diminutive skillet beside it. Corn bread and tea and sugar came from the capacious pockets of the saddle. Billy and his missionary made a good meal beneath the wide bright quiet of the sky.

When the corn chop was finished Billy let his long lashes droop lower and lower, and his nose go down and down until it almost touched the ground, dreaming of more corn chop, and happy in having his wants supplied. But his master, stretched at full length upon the ground with hat drawn over his eyes, could not lose himself in sleep for a second. His thoughts were upon the jewelled whip, and by and by he reached his hand out for it, and shoving back his hat lay watching the glinting of lights within the precious heart of the topaz, as the sun caught and tangled its beams in the sharp facets of the cutting. He puzzled his mind to know how the whip came to be in the desert, and what was meant by it. One reads life by details in that wide and lonely land. This whip might mean something. But what?

At last he dropped his hand and sitting up with his upward glance he said aloud:

"Father, if there's any reason why I ought to look for the owner, guide me."

He spoke as if the One he addressed were always present in his consciousness, and they were on terms of the closest intimacy.

He sprang up then and began putting the things together, as

if the burden of the responsibility were upon One fully able to bear it.

They were soon on their way again, Billy swinging along with the full realization of the nearness of home.

The way now led towards hazy blue lines of mesas with crags and ridges here and there. Across the valley, looking like a cloud-shadow, miles distant lay a long black streak, the line of the gorge of the canyon. Its dim presence seemed to grow on the missionary's thought as he drew nearer. He had not been to that canyon for more than a month. There were a few scattered Indians living with their families here and there in corners where there was a little soil. The thought of them drew him now. He must make out to go to them soon. If it were not that Billy had been so far he would go up there this afternoon. But the horse needed rest if the man did not, and there was of course no real hurry about the matter. He would go perhaps in the morning. Meantime it would be good to get to his own fireside once more and attend to a few letters that should be written. He was invited to the fort that night for dinner. There was to be some kind of a frolic, some visitors from the East. He had said he would come if he reached home in time. He probably would, but the idea was not attractive just now. He would rather rest and read and go to sleep early. But then, of course he would go. Such opportunities were none too frequent in this lonely land, though in his present mood the gay doings at the fort did not appeal to him strongly; besides it meant a ride of ten miles further. However, of course he would go. He fell to musing over the whip again, and in due time he arrived at his own home, a little one-roomed shanty with a chimney at the back and four big windows. At the extreme end of the fenced enclosure about the structure was a little shed for Billy, and all about was the vast plain dotted with bushes and weeds, with its panorama of mountain and hill, valley and gorge. It was beautiful, but it was desolate. There were neighbours, a few, but they lived at magnificent distances.

"We ought to have a dog, Billy! Why don't we get a dog to welcome us home?" said Brownleigh, slapping the horse's neck affectionately as he sprang from the saddle; "but then a dog would go along with us, wouldn't he, so there'd be three of us to come home instead of two, and that wouldn't do any good. Chickens? How would that do? But the coyotes would steal them. I guess we'll have to get along with each other, old fellow.''

The horse, relieved of his saddle, gave a shake of comfort as a man might stretch himself after a weary journey, and trotted into his shed. Brownleigh made him comfortable and turned to go to the house.

As he walked along by the fence he caught sight of a small dark object hanging on a sage-bush a short distance from the front of his house. It seemed to move slightly, and he stopped and watched it a second thinking it might be some animal caught in the bush, or in hiding. It seemed to stir again as objects watched intently often will, and springing over the rail fence Brownleigh went to investigate. Nothing in that country was left to uncertainty. Men liked to know what was about them.

As he neared the bush, however, the object took on a tangible form and colour, and coming closer he picked it up and turned it over clumsily in his hand. A little velvet riding cap, undoubtedly a lady's, with the name of a famous New York costumer wrought in silk letters in the lining. Yes, there was no question about its being a lady's cap, for a long gleaming golden hair, with an undoubted tendency to curl, still clung to the velvet. A sudden embarrassment filled him, as though he had been handling too intimately another's property unawares. He raised his eyes and shaded them with his hand to look across the landscape, if perchance the owner might be at hand, though even as he did so he felt a conviction that the little velvet cap belonged to the owner of the whip which he still held in his other hand. H.R. Where was H.R., and who could she be?

For some minutes he stood thinking it out, locating the exact spot in his memory where he had found the whip. It had not been on any regular trail. That was strange. He stooped to see if there were any further evidences of passers-by, but the slight breeze had softly covered all definite marks. He was satisfied, however, after examining the ground about for some distance either way, that there could have been but one horse. He was wise in the lore of the trail. By certain little things that he saw or did not see he came to this conclusion.

Just as he was turning to go back to his cabin he came to a

halt again with an exclamation of wonder, for there close at his feet, half hidden under a bit of sage, lay a small shell comb. He stooped and picked it up in triumph.

"I declare, I have quite a collection," he said aloud. "Are there any more? By these tokens I may be able to find her after all." And he started with a definite purpose and searched the ground for several rods ahead, then going back and taking a slightly different direction, he searched again and yet again, looking back each time to get his bearings from the direction where he had found the whip, arguing that the horse must likely have taken a pretty straight line and gone at a rapid pace.

He was rewarded at last by finding two shell hairpins, and near them a single hoof print, that, sheltered by a heavy growth of sage, had escaped the obliteration of the wind. This he knelt and studied carefully, taking in all the details of size and shape and direction; then, finding no more hairpins or combs, he carefully put his booty into his pocket and hurried back to the cabin, his brow knit in deep thought.

"Father, is this Thy leading?" He paused at the door and looked up. He opened the door and stepped within. The restfulness of the place called to him to stay.

There was the wide fireplace with a fire laid all ready for the touch of a match that would bring the pleasant blaze to dispel the loneliness of the place. There was the easy chair, his one luxury, with its leather cushions and reclining back; his slippers on the floor close by; the little table with its well-trimmed student lamp, his college paper and the one magazine that kept him in touch with the world freshly arrived before he left for his recent trip, and still unopened. How they called to him! Yet when he laid the whip upon the magazine the slanting ray of sun that entered by the door caught the glory of the topaz and sent it scintillating, and somehow the magazine lost its power to hold him.

One by one he laid his trophies down beside the whip; the velvet cap, the hairpins and the little comb, and then stood back startled with the wonder of it and looked about his bachelor quarters.

It was a pleasant spot, far lovelier than its weather-stained exterior would lead one to suppose. A Navajo blanket hung upon one wall above the bed, and another enwrapped and

16

completely covered the bed itself, making a spot of colour in the room, and giving an air of luxury. Two quaint rugs of Indian workmanship upon the floor, one in front of the bed, the other before the fireplace where one's feet would rest when sitting in the big chair, did much to hide the discrepancies of the ugly floor. A rough set of shelves at the side of the fireplace handy to reach from the easy chair were filled with treasures of great minds, the books he loved well, all he could afford to bring with him, a few commentaries, not many, an encyclopedia, a little biography, a few classics, botany, biology, astronomy and a much worn Bible. On the wall above was a large card catalogue of Indian words; and around the room were some of his own pencil drawings of plants and animals.

Over in the opposite end of the room from the bed was a table covered with white oilcloth; and on the wall behind, the cupboard which held his dishes, and his stock of provisions. It was a pleasant spot and well ordered, for he never liked to leave his quarters in disarray lest some one might enter during his absence, or come back with him. Besides, it was pleasanter so to return to it. A rough closet of goodly proportions held his clothes, his trunk, and any other stores.

He stood and looked about it now and then let his eyes travel back to those small feminine articles on the little table beside him. It gave him a strange sensation. What if they belonged there? What if the owner of them lived there, was coming in in a minute now to meet him? How would it seem? What would she be like? For just an instant he let himself dream, and reaching out touched the velvet of the cap, then took it in his hand and smoothed its silken surface. A faint perfume of another world seemed to steal from its texture, and to linger on his hands. He drew a breath of wonder and laid it down; then with a start he came to himself. Suppose she did belong, and were out somewhere and he did not know where? Suppose something had happened to her—the horse run away, thrown her somewhere perhaps,—or she might have strayed away from a camp and lost her way—or been frightened?

These might be all foolish fantasies of a weary brain, but the man knew he could not rest until he had at least made an attempt to find out. He sank down in the big chair for a moment to think it out and closed his eyes, making swift plans.

Billy must have a chance to rest a little; a fagged horse could not accomplish much if the journey were far and the need for haste. He could not go for an hour yet. And there would be preparations to make. He must repack the saddle-bags with feed for Billy, food for himself and a possible stranger, restoratives, and a simple remedy or two in case of accident. These were articles he always took with him on long journeys. He considered taking his camping tent but that would mean the wagon, and they could not go so rapidly with that. He must not load Billy heavily, after the miles he had already come. But he could take a bit of canvas strapped to the saddle, and a small blanket. Of course it might be but a wild goose chase after all—yet he could not let his impressions go unheeded.

Then there was the fort. In case he found the lady and restored her property in time he might be able to reach the fort by evening. He must take that into consideration also.

With alacrity he arose and went about his preparations, soon having his small baggage in array. His own toilet came next. A bath and fresh clothing; then, clean shaven and ready, all but his coat, he flung himself upon his bed for ten minutes of absolute relaxation, after which he felt himself quite fit for the expedition. Springing up he put on coat and hat, gathered up with reverent touch the bits of things he had found, locked his cabin and went out to Billy, a lump of sugar in his hand.

"Billy, old fellow, we're under orders to march again," he said apologetically, and Billy answered with a neigh of plea-sure, submitting to the saddle as though he were quite ready for anything required of him.

"Now, Father," said the missionary with his upward look, "show us the way."

So, taking the direction from the hoof print in the sand, Billy and his master sped away once more into the westering light of the desert towards the long black shadowed entrance of the canyon.

III

The Desert

Hazel, as she was borne along, her lovely hair streaming in the wind and lashing her across the face and eyes now and again, breath coming painfully, eyes smarting, fingers aching in the vise-like hold she was compelled to keep upon the saddle, began to wonder just how long she could hold out. It seemed to her it was a matter of minutes only when she must let go and be whirled into space while the tempestuous steed sped on and left her.

Nothing like this motion had ever come into her experience before. She had been run away with once, but that was like a cradle to this tornado of motion. She had been frightened before, but never like this. The blood pounded in her head and eyes until it seemed it would burst forth, and now and again the surging of it through her ears gave the sensation of drowning, yet on and on she went. It was horrible to have no bridle, and nothing to say about where she should go, no chance to control her horse. It was like being on an express train with the engineer dead in his cab and no way to get to the brakes. They must stop sometime and what then? Death seemed inevitable, and yet as the mad rush continued she almost wished it might come and end the horror of this ride.

It seemed hours before she began to realize that the horse was no longer going at quite such a breakneck speed, or else she was growing accustomed to the motion and getting her breath, she could not quite be sure which. But little by little she perceived that the mad flying had settled into a long lope. The pony evidently had no intention of stopping and it was plain that he had some distinct place in mind to which he was going as straight and determinedly as any human being ever laid out a course and forged ahead in it. There was that about his whole beastly contour that showed it was perfectly useless to try to deter him from it or to turn him aside.

When her breath came less painfully, Hazel made a fitful little attempt to drop a quiet word of reason into his ear.

"Nice pony, nice, good pony——!" she soothed, but the wind caught her voice and flung it aside as it had flung her cap a few moments before, and the pony only laid his ears back and fled stolidly on.

She gathered her forces again.

"Nice pony! Whoa, sir!" she cried, a little louder than the last time and trying to make her voice sound firm and commanding.

But the pony had no intention of "whoaing," and though she repeated the command many times, her voice growing each time more firm and normal, he only showed the whites of his eyes at her and continued doggedly on his way.

She saw it was useless; and the tears, usually with her under fine control, came streaming down her white cheeks.

"Pony, good horse, *dear* pony, won't you stop!" she cried and her words ended with a sob. But still the pony kept on.

The desert fled about her yet seemed to grow no shorter ahead, and the dark line of cloud mystery, with the towering mountains beyond, were no nearer than when she first started. It seemed much like riding on a rocking-horse, one never got anywhere, only no rocking-horse flew at such a speed.

Yet she realized now that the pace was much modified from what it had been at first, and the pony's motion was not hard. If she had not been so stiff and sore in every joint and muscle with the terrible tension she had kept up the riding would not have been at all bad. But she was conscious of most terrible weariness, a longing to drop down on the sand of the desert and rest, not caring whether she ever went on again or not. She had never felt such terrible weariness in her life.

She could hold on now with one hand, and relax the muscles of the other a little. She tried with one hand presently to do something with that sweeping pennant of hair that lashed her in the face so unexpectedly now and then, but could only succeed in twisting it about her neck and tucking the ends into the neck of her riding habit; and from this frail binding it soon slipped free again.

She was conscious of the heat of the sun on her bare head, the smarting of her eyes. The pain in her chest was subsiding, and she could breathe freely again, but her heart felt tired, so tired, and she wanted to lie down and cry. Would she never get anywhere and be helped?

How soon would her father and brother miss her and come after her? When she dared she looked timidly behind, and then again more lingeringly, but there was nothing to be seen but the same awful stretch of distance with mountains of bright colour in the boundaries everywhere; not a living thing but herself and the pony to be seen. It was awful. Somewhere between herself and the mountains behind was the place she had started from, but the bright sun shone steadily, hotly down and shimmered back again from the bright earth, and nothing broke the awful repose of the lonely space. It was as if she had suddenly been caught up and flung out into a world where was no other living being.

Why did they not come after her? Surely, surely, pretty soon she would see them coming. They would spur their horses on when they found she had been run away with. Her father and brother would not leave her long in this horrible plight.

Then it occurred to her that her father and brother had been for some time out of sight ahead before she began her race. They would not know she was gone, at once; but of course Mr. Hamar would do something. He would not leave her helpless. The habit of years of trusting him assured her of that. For the instant she had forgotten the cause of her flight. Then suddenly she remembered it with sickening thought. He who had been to her a brave fine hero, suffering daily through the carelessness of a wife who did not understand him, had stepped down from his pedestal and become the lowest of the low. He had dared to kiss her! He had said he would marry her—he,—a married man! Her whole soul revolted against him again, and now she was glad she had run away—glad the horse had taken her so far—glad she had shown him how terrible the whole thing looked to her. She was even glad that her father and brother were far away too, for the present, until she should adjust herself to life once more. How could she have faced them after what happened? How could she ever live in the same world with that man again,—that fallen

21

hero? How could she ever have thought so much of him? She had almost worshipped him, and had been so pleased when he had seemed to enjoy her company, and complimented her by telling her she had whiled away a weary hour for him! And he? He had been meaning—*this*—all the time! He had looked at her with that thought in his mind! Oh—awful degradation!

There was something so revolting in the memory of his voice and face as he told her that she closed her eyes and shuddered as she recalled it, and once more the tears went coursing down her cheeks and she sobbed aloud, piteously, her head bowing lower and lower over the pony's neck, her bright hair falling down about her shoulders and beating against the animal's breast and knees as he ran, her stiffened fingers clutching his mane to keep her balance, her whole weary little form drooping over his neck in a growing exhaustion, her entire being swept by alternate waves of anger, revulsion and fear.

Perhaps all this had its effect on the beast; perhaps somewhere in his make-up there lay a spot, call it instinct or what you please, that vibrated in response to the distress of the human creature he carried. Perhaps the fact that she was in trouble drew his sympathy, wicked little willful imp though he usually was. Certain it is that he began to slacken his pace decidedly, until at last he was walking, and finally stopped short and turned his head about with a troubled neigh as if to ask her what was the matter.

The sudden cessation of the motion almost threw her from her seat; and with new fear gripping her heart she clutched the pony's mane the tighter and looked about her trembling. She was conscious more than anything else of the vast spaces about her in every direction, of the loneliness of the spot, and her own desolate condition. She had wanted the horse to stop and let her get down to solid ground, and now that he had done so and she might dismount a great horror filled her and she dared not. But with the lessening of the need for keeping up the tense strain of nerve and muscle, she suddenly began to feel that she could not sit up any longer, that she must lie down, let go this awful strain, stop this uncontrollable trembling which was quivering all over her body.

The pony, too, seemed wondering, impatient that she did

not dismount at once. He turned his nose towards her again with a questioning snuff and snort, and showed the wicked whites of his eyes in wild perplexity. Then a panic seized her. What if he should start to run again? She would surely be thrown this time, for her strength was almost gone. She must get down and in some way gain possession of the bridle. With the bridle she might perhaps hope to guide his movements, and make further wild riding impossible.

Slowly, painfully, guardedly, she took her boot from the stirrup and slipped to the ground. Her cramped feet refused to hold her weight for the moment and she tottered and went into a little heap on the ground. The pony, feeling his duty for the present done, sidled away from her and began cropping the grass hungrily.

The girl sank down wearily at full length upon the ground and for a moment it seemed to her she could never rise again. She was too weary to lift her hand or to move the foot that was twisted under her into a more comfortable position, too weary to even think. Then suddenly the sound of the animal moving steadily away from her roused her to the necessity of securing him. If he should get away in this wide desolation she would be helpless indeed.

She gathered her flagging energy and got painfully upon her feet. The horse was nearly a rod away, and moving slowly, steadily, as he ate, with now and then a restless lifting of his head to look off into the distance and take a few determined steps before he stopped for another bite. That horse had something on his mind and was going straight towards it. She felt that he cared little what became of her. She must look out for herself. This was something she had never had to do before; but the instinct came with the need.

Slowly, tremblingly, feeling her weakness, she stole towards him, a bunch of grass in her hand she had plucked as she came, holding it obviously as she had fed a lump of sugar or an apple to her finely groomed mare in New York. But the grass she held was like all the grass about him, and the pony had not been raised a pet. He tossed his nose energetically and scornfully as she drew near and hastened on a pace or two.

Cautiously she came on again talking to him gently, pleadingly, complimentarily: "Nice good horsey! Pretty pony so he was!" But he only edged away again.

And so they went on for some little way until Hazel almost despaired of catching him at all, and was becoming more and more aware of the vastness of the universe about her, and the smallness of her own being.

At last, however, her fingers touched the bridle, she felt the pony's quick jerk, strained every muscle to hold on, and found she had conquered. He was in her hands. For how long was a question, for he was strong enough to walk away and drag her by the bridle perhaps, and she knew little about tricks of management. Moreover her muscles were so flabby and sore with the long ride that she was ill-fitted to cope with the wise and wicked little beast. She dreaded to get upon his back again, and doubted if she could if she tried, but it seemed the only way to get anywhere, or to keep company with the pony, for she could not hope to detain him by mere physical force if he decided otherwise.

She stood beside him for a moment, looking about her over the wide distance. Everything looked alike, and different from anything she had ever seen before. She must certainly get on that pony's back, for her fear of the desert became constantly greater. It was almost as if it would snatch her away in a moment more if she stayed there longer, and carry her into vaster realms of space where her soul would be lost in infinitude. She had never been possessed by any such feeling before and it frightened her unreasoningly.

Turning to the pony, she measured the space from the ground to the queer saddle and wondered how people mounted such things without a groom. When she had mounted that morning it had been Milton Hamar's strong arm that swung her into the saddle, and his hand that held her foot for the instant of her spring. The memory of it now sent a shudder of dislike over her whole body. If she had known, he never should have touched her! The blood mounted uncomfortably into her tired face, and made her conscious of the heat of the day, and of a burning thirst. She must go on and get to some water somewhere. She could not stand this much longer.

Carefully securing the bridle over her arm she reached up and took hold of the saddle, doubtfully at first, and then desperately; tried to reach the stirrup with one foot, failed and tried again; and then wildly struggling, jumping, kicking, she vainly sought to climb back to the saddle. But the pony was not accustomed to such a demonstration at mounting and he strongly objected. Tossing his head he reared and dashed off, almost throwing the girl to the ground and frightening her terribly.

Nevertheless the desperation of her situation gave her strength for a fresh trial, and she struggled up again, and almost gained her seat, when the pony began a series of circles which threw her down and made her dizzy with trying to keep up with him.

Thus they played the desperate game for half an hour more. Twice the girl lost the bridle and had to get it again by stealthy wiles, and once she was almost on the point of giving up, so utterly exhausted was she.

But the pony was thirsty too, and he must have decided that the quickest way to water would be to let her mount; for finally with lifted head he stood stock still and let her struggle up his side, and at last, well-nigh falling from sheer weariness, she sat astonished that she had accomplished it. She was on his back, and she would never dare to get down again, she thought, until she got some where to safety. But now the animal, his courage renewed by the bite he had taken, started snorting off at a rapid pace once more, very nearly upsetting his rider at the start, and almost losing her the bridle once more. She sat trembling, and gripping bridle and saddle for some time, having enough to do to keep her seat without trying to direct her bearer, and then she saw before her a sudden descent, steep but not very long, and at its bottom a great puddle of dirty water. The pony paused only an instant on the brink and then began the descent. The girl cried out with fear, but managed to keep her seat, and the impatient animal was soon ankle deep in the water drinking long and blissfully.

Hazel sat looking in dismay about her. The water-hole seemed to be entirely surrounded by steep banks like that they had descended, and there was no way out except to return. Could the horse climb up with her on his back? And could she keep her seat? She grew cold with fear at the thought, for all her riding experience had been on the level, and she had become more and more conscious of her flagging strength.

25

Besides, the growing thirst was becoming awful. Oh, for just one drop of that water that the pony was enjoying! Black and dirty as it was she felt she could drink it. But it was out of her reach and she dared not get down. Suddenly a thought came to her. She would wet her handkerchief and moisten her lips with that. If she stooped over quite carefully she might be able to let it down far enough to touch the water.

She pulled the small bit of linen from the tiny pocket of her habit and the pony, as if to help her, waded into the water farther until her skirt almost touched it. Now she found that by putting her arm about the pony's neck she could dip most of her handkerchief in the water, and dirty as it was it was most refreshing to bathe her face and hands and wrists and moisten her lips.

But the pony when he had his fill had no mind to tarry, and with a splash, a plunge and a wallow that gave the girl an unexpected shower bath, he picked his way out of the hole and up the rocky side of the descent, while she clung frightened to the saddle and wondered if she could possibly hang on until they were up on the mesa again. The dainty handkerchief dropped in the flight floated pitifully on the muddy water, another bit of comfort left behind.

But when they were up and away again, what with the fright, and the fact that they had come out of the hole on the opposite side from that which they had entered it, the girl had lost all sense of direction, and everywhere stretched away one vast emptiness edged with mountains that stood out clear, cold and unfriendly.

The whole atmosphere of the earth seemed to have changed while they were down at the drinking hole, for now the shadows were long and had almost a menacing attitude as they crept along or leaped sideways after the travellers. Hazel noticed with a startled glance at the sky that the sun was low and would soon be down. And that of course where the sun hung like a great burning opal must be the west, but that told her nothing, for the sun had been high in the heavens when they had started, and she had taken no note of direction. East, west, north or south were all one to her in her happy care-free life that she had hitherto led. She tried to puzzle it out and remember which way they had turned from the railroad but grew more bewildered, and the brilliant display in the west flamed alarmingly as she realized that night was coming on and she was lost on a great desert with only a wild tired little pony for company, hungry and thirsty and weary beyond anything she had ever dreamed before.

They had been going down into a broad valley for some little time, which made the night seem even nearer. Hazel would have turned her horse back and tried to retrace her steps, but that he would not, for try as she might, and turn him as she would he circled about and soon was in the same course again, so that now the tired hands could only hold the reins stiffly and submit to be carried where the pony willed. It was quite evident he had a destination in view, and knew the way thereto. Hazel had read of the instinct of animals. She began to hope that he would presently bring her to a human habitation where she would find help to get to her father once more.

But suddenly even the glory of the dying sun was lost as the horse entered the dimness of the canyon opening, whose high walls of red stone, rising solemnly on either hand, were serrated here and there with long transverse lines of grasses and tree-ferns growing in the crevices, and higher up appeared the black openings of caves mysterious and fearsome in twilight gloom. The way ahead loomed darkly. Somewhere from out the memories of her childhood came a phrase from the church-service to which she had never given conscious attention, but which flashed vividly to mind now: "Though I walk through the valley of the shadow—the Valley of the Shadow!" Surely this must be it. She wished she could remember the rest of it. What could it have meant? She shivered visibly, and looked about her with wild eyes.

The cottonwoods and oaks grew thickly at the base of the cliffs, almost concealing them sometimes, and above the walls rose dark and towering. The way was rough and slippery, filled with great boulders and rocks, around which the pony picked his way without regard to the branches of trees that swept her face and caught in her long hair as they went by.

Vainly she strove to guide him back, but he turned only to whirl again, determinedly. Somewhere in the deep gloom ahead he had a destination and no mere girl was to deter him from reaching it as soon as possible. It was plain to his horse-mind that his rider did not know what she wanted, and he did, so there were no two ways about it. He intended to go back to his old master as straight and as fast as he could get there. This canyon was the shortest cut and through this canyon he meant to walk whether she liked it or not.

Further and further into the gloom they penetrated, and the girl, frenzied with fear, cried out with the wild hope that some one might be near and come to her rescue. But the gloomy aisle of the canyon caught up her voice and echoed it far and high, until it came back to her in a volume of sepulchral sound that filled her with a nameless dread and made her fear to open her lips again. It was as if she had by her cry awakened the evil spirit who inhabited the canyon and set it searching for the intruder. "Help! Help!" How the words rolled and returned upon her trembling senses until she quaked and quivered with their echoes!

On went the pony into the deepening shadows, and each moment the darkness shut down more impenetrably, until the girl could only close her eyes, lower her head as much as possible to escape the branches—and pray.

Then suddenly, from above where the distant sky gave a line of light and a single star had appeared to pierce the dusk like a great jewel on a lady's gown, there arose a sound; blood-curdling and hideous, high, hollow, far-echoing, chilling her soul with horror and causing her heart to stand still with fear. She had heard it once before, a night or two ago, when their train had stopped in a wide desert for water or repairs or something and the porter of the car had told her it was coyotes. It had been distant then, and weird and interesting to think of being so near real live wild animals. She had peered from the safety of her berth behind the silken curtains and fancied she saw shadowy forms steal over the plain under the moonlight. But it was a very different thing to hear the sound now, out alone among their haunts, with no weapon and none to protect her. The awfulness of her situation almost took away her senses.

Still she held to the saddle, weak and trembling, expecting every minute to be her last; and the horrid howling of the coyotes continued.

Down below the trail somewhere she could hear the soft trickling of water with maddening distinctness now and then.

Oh, if she could but quench this terrible thirst! The pony was somewhat refreshed with his grass and his drink of water, but the girl, whose life up to this day had never known a want unsatisfied, was faint with hunger and burning with thirst, and this unaccustomed demand upon her strength was fast bringing it to its limit.

The darkness in the canyon grew deeper, and more stars clustered out overhead; but far, so very far away! The coyotes seemed just a shadow removed all about and above. Her senses were swimming. She could not be sure just where they were. The horse slipped and stumbled on in the darkness, and she forgot to try to turn him from his purpose.

By and by she grew conscious that the way was leading upward again. They were scrambling over rough places, large rocks in the way, trees growing close to the trail, and the pony seemed not to be able to avoid them, or perhaps he didn't care. The howling of the coyotes was growing clearer every minute but somehow her fear of them was deadened, as her fear of all else. She was lying low upon the pony, clinging to his neck, too faint to cry out, too weak to stop the tears that slowly wet his mane. Then suddenly she was caught in the embrace of a low hanging branch, her hair tangled about its roughness. The pony struggled to gain his uncertain footing, the branch held her fast and the pony scrambled on, leaving his helpless rider behind him in a little huddled heap upon the rocky trail, swept from the saddle by the tough old branch.

The pony stopped a moment upon a bit of shelving rock he had with difficulty gained, and looked back with a troubled snort, but the huddled heap in the darkness below him gave forth no sign of life, and after another snort and a half neigh of warning the pony turned and scrambled on, up and up till he gained the mesa above.

The late moon rose and hunted its way through the canyon till it found the gold of her hair spread about on the rocky way, and touched her sweet unconscious face with the light of cold beauty; the coyotes howled on in solemn chorus, and still the little figure lay quiet and unconscious of her situation.

IV

The Quest

John Brownleigh reached the water-hole at sunset, and while he waited for his horse to drink he meditated on what he would do next. If he intended to go to the fort for dinner he should turn at once sharply to the right and ride hard, unless he was willing to be late. The lady at the fort liked to have her guests on hand promptly, he knew.

The sun was down. It had left long splashes of crimson and gold in the west, and their reflection was shimmering over the muddy water below him so that Billy looked as if he quaffed the richest wine from a golden cup, as he satisfied his thirst contentedly.

But as the missionary watched the painted water and tried to decide his course, suddenly his eye caught a bit of white something floating, half clinging to a twig at the edge of the water, a bit of thin transparentness, with delicate lacy edge. It startled him in that desert place much as the jewel in its golden setting in the sand had startled him that morning.

With an exclamation of surprise he stooped over, picked up the little wet handkerchief and held it out—dainty, white and fine, and in spite of its wet condition sending forth its violet breath to the senses of a man who had been in the wilds of the desert for three years. It spoke of refinement and culture and a world he had left behind him in the East.

There was a tiny letter embroidered in the corner, but already the light was growing too dim to read it, and though he held it up and looked through it and felt the embroidery with his finger-tip he could not be sure that it was either of the letters that had been engraved on the whip.

Nevertheless, the little white messenger determined his course. He searched the edge of the water-hole for hoof prints as well as the dying light would reveal, then mounted Billy with decision at once and took up his quest where he had almost abandoned it. He was convinced that a lady was out alone in the desert somewhere.

It was long past midnight when Billy and the missionary came upon the pony, high on the mesa, grazing. The animal had evidently felt the need for food and rest before proceeding further, and was perhaps a little uneasy about that huddled form in the darkness he had left.

Billy and the pony were soon hobbled and left to feed together while the missionary, all thought of his own need of rest forgotten, began a systematic search for the missing rider. He first carefully examined the pony and saddle. The saddle somehow reminded him of Shag Bunce, but the pony was a stranger to him; neither could he make out the letter of the brand in the pale moonlight. However, it might be a new animal, just purchased and not yet branded—or there might be a thousand explanations. The thought of Shag Bunce reminded him of the handsome private car he had seen upon the track that morning. But even if a party had gone out to ride how would one of them get separated? Surely no lady would venture over the desert alone, not a stranger at any rate.

Still in the silver and black of the shadowed night he searched on, and not until the rosy light of dawning began to flush and grow in the east did he come to stand at the top of the canyon where he could look down and see the girl, her green riding habit blending darkly with the dark forms of the trees still in shadow, the gold of her hair glinted with the early light, and her white, white face turned upward.

He lost no time in climbing down to her side, dreading what he might find. Was she dead? What had happened to her? It was a perilous spot where she lay, and the dangers that might have harmed her had been many. The sky grew pink, and tinted all the clouds with rose as he knelt beside the still form.

A moment served to convince him that she was still alive; even in the half darkness he could see the drawn, weary look of her face. Poor child! Poor little girl, lost on the desert! He was glad, glad he had come to find her.

He gathered her in his strong arms and bore her upward to the light.

Laying her in a sheltered spot he quickly brought water, bathed her face and forced a stimulant between the white lips. He chafed her cold little hands, blistered with the bridle, gave her more stimulant, and was rewarded by seeing a faint colour steal into the lips and cheeks. Finally the white lids fluttered open for a second and gave him a glimpse of great dark eyes in which was still mirrored the horror and fright of the night.

He gave her another draught, and hastened to prepare a more comfortable resting place, bringing the canvas from Billy's pack, and one or two other little articles that might make for comfort, among them a small hot water bottle. When he had her settled on the canvas with sweet ferns and grass underneath for a pillow and his own blanket spread over her he set about gathering wood for a fire, and soon he had water boiling in his tin cup, enough to fill the rubber bottle. When he put it in her cold hands she opened her eyes again wonderingly. He smiled reassuringly and she nestled down contentedly with the comfort of the warmth. She was too weary to question or know aught save that relief from a terrible horror was come at last.

The next time he came to her it was with a cup of strong beef tea which he held to her lips and coaxed her to swallow. When it was finished she lay back and slept again with a long drawn trembling sigh that was almost like a sob, and the heart of the young man was shaken to its depths over the agony through which she must have passed. Poor child, poor little child!

He busied himself with making their temporary camp as comfortable as possible, and looking after the needs of the horses, then coming back to his patient he stood looking down at her as she slept, wondering what he ought to do next.

They were a long distance from any human habitation. Whatever made the pony take this lonely trail was a puzzle. It led to a distant Indian settlement, and doubtless the animal was returning to his former master, but how had it come that the rider had not turned him back?

Then he looked down at the frail girl asleep on the ground and grew grave as he thought of the perils through which she had passed alone and unguarded. The exquisite delicacy of her face touched him as the vision of an angelic being might have done, and for an instant he forgot everything in the wonder with which her beauty filled him; the lovely outline of the profile as it rested lightly against her raised arm, the fineness and length of her wealth of hair, like spun gold in the glint of the sunshine that was just peering over the rim of the mountain, the clearness of her skin, so white and different from the women in that region, the pitiful droop of the sweet lips showing utter exhaustion. His heart went out from him with longing to comfort her, guard her, and bring her back to happiness. A strange, joyful tenderness for her filled him as he looked, so that he could scarcely draw his gaze from her face. Then all at once it came over him that she would not like a stranger thus to stand and gaze upon her helplessness, and with quick reverence he turned his eyes away towards the sky.

It was a peculiar morning, wonderfully beautiful. The clouds were tinted pink almost like a sunset and lasted so for over an hour, as if the dawn were coming gently that it might not waken her who slept.

Brownleigh, with one more glance to see if his patient was comfortable, went softly away to gather wood, bring more water, and make various little preparations for a breakfast later when she should waken. In an hour he tiptoed back to see if all was going well, and stooping laid a practiced finger on the delicate wrist to note the flutter of her pulse. He could count it with care, feeble, as if the heart had been under heavy strain, but still growing steadier on the whole. She was doing well to sleep. It was better than any medicine he could administer.

Meantime, he must keep a sharp lookout for travellers. They were quite off the trail here, and the trail was an old one anyway and almost disused. There was little likelihood of many passers. It might be days before any one came that way. There was no human habitation within call, and he dared not leave his charge to go in search of help to carry her back to civilization again. He must just wait here till she was able to travel.

It occurred to him to wonder where she belonged and how she came to be thus alone, and whether it was not altogether probable that a party of searchers might be out soon with

33

some kind of a conveyance to carry her home. He must keep a sharp lookout and signal any passing rider.

To this end he moved away from the sleeping girl as far as he dared leave her, and uttered a long, clear call occasionally, but no answer came.

He dared not use his rifle for signalling lest he run out of ammunition which he might need before he got back with his charge. However, he felt it wise to combine hunting with signalling, and when a rabbit hurried across his path not far away he shot it, and the sound echoed out in the clear morning, but no answering signal came.

After he had shot two rabbits and dressed them ready for dinner when his guest should wake, he replenished the fire, set the rabbits to roasting on a curious little device of his own, and lay down on the opposite side of the fire. He was weary beyond expression himself, but he never thought of it once. The excitement of the occasion kept him up. He lay still marvelling at the strangeness of his position, and wondering what would be revealed when the girl should awake. He almost dreaded to have her do so lest she should not be as perfect as she looked asleep. His heart was in a tumult of wonder over her, and of thankfulness that he had found her before some terrible fate had overtaken her.

As he lay there resting, filled with an exalted joy, his mind wantered to the longings of the day before, the little adobe home of his co-labourer which he had left, its homeyness and joy; his own loneliness and longing for companionship. Then he looked shyly towards the tree shade where the glint of golden hair and the dark line of his blanket were all he could see of the girl he had found in the wilderness. What if his Father had answered his prayer and sent her to him! What miracle of joy! A thrill of tenderness passed through him and he pressed his hands over his closed eyes in a kind of ecstasy.

What foolishness! Dreams, of course! He tried to sober himself but he could not keep from thinking how it would seem to have this lovely girl enthroned in his little shack, ready to share his joys and comfort his sorrows; to be beloved and guarded and tenderly cared for by him.

A stir of the old blanket and a softly drawn sigh brought this delicious reverie to a close, and himself to his feet flushing cold and hot at thought of facing her awake.

She had turned over towards him slightly, her cheeks flushed with sleep. One hand was thrown back over her head, and the sun caught and flashed the sparkle of jewels into his eyes, great glory-clear gems like drops of morning dew when the sun is new upon them, and the flash of the jewels told him once more what he had known before that here was a daughter of another world than his. They seemed to hurt him as he looked, those costly gems, for they pierced to his heart and told him they were set on a wall of separation which might rise forever between her and himself.

Then suddenly he came to himself and was the missionary again, with his senses all on the alert, and a keen realization that it was high noon and his patient was waking up. He must have slept himself although he thought he had been broad awake all the time. The hour had come for action and he must put aside the foolish thoughts that had crowded in when his weary brain was unable to cope with the cool facts of life. Of course all this stuff and nonsense that he had been dreaming. He must do his duty by this needy one now.

Stepping softly he brought a cup of water that he had placed in the shade to keep cool, and stood beside the girl, speaking quietly, as though he had been her nurse for years.

"Wouldn't you like a drink of water?" he asked.

The girl opened her eyes and looked up at him bewildered.

"Oh, yes," she said eagerly, though her voice was very weak. "Oh, yes,—I'm so thirsty.—I thought we never would get anywhere!"

She let him lift her head, and drank eagerly, then sank back exhausted and closed her eyes. He almost thought she was going to sleep again.

"Wouldn't you like something to eat?" he asked. "Dinner is almost ready. Do you think you can sit up to eat or would you rather lie still?"

"Dinner!" she said languidly; "but I thought it was night. Did I dream it all, and how did I get here? I don't remember this place."

She looked around curiously and then closed her eyes as if the effort were almost too much.

"Oh, I feel so queer and tired, as if I never wanted to move again," she murmured.

"Don't move," he commanded. "Wait until you've had something to eat. I'll bring it at once."

He brought a cup of steaming hot beef extract with little broken bits of biscuit from a small tin box in the pack, and fed it to her a spoonful at a time.

"Who are you?" she asked as she swallowed the last spoonful, and opened her eyes, which had been closed most of the time, while he fed her, as if she were too tired to keep them open.

"Oh, I'm just the missionary. Brownleigh's my name. Now don't talk until you've had the rest of your dinner. I'll bring it in a minute. I want to make you a cup of tea, but you see I have to wash this cup first. The supply of dishes is limited." His genial smile and hearty words reassured her and she smiled and submitted.

"A missionary!" she mused and opened her eyes furtively to watch him as he went about his task. A missionary! She had never seen a missionary before, to her knowledge. She had fancied them always quite a different species, plain old maids with hair tightly drawn behind their ears and a poke bonnet with little white lawn strings.

This was a man, young, strong, engaging, and handsome as a fine piece of bronze. The brown flannel shirt he wore fitted easily over well knit muscles and exactly matched the brown of the abundant wavy hair in which the morning sun was setting glints of gold as he knelt before the fire and deftly completed his cookery. His soft wide-brimmed felt hat pushed far back on the head, the corduroy trousers, leather chaps and belt with brace of pistols all fitted into the picture and made the girl feel that she had suddenly left the earth where she had heretofore lived and been dropped into an unknown land with a strong kind angel to look after her.

A missionary! Then of course she needn't be afraid of him. As she studied his face she knew that she couldn't possibly have been afraid of that face anyway, unless, perhaps, she had ventured to disobey its owner's orders. He had a strong, firm chin, and his lips though kindly in their curve looked decided as though they were not to be trifled with. On the whole if this was a missionary then she must change her ideas of missionaries from this time forth.

She watched his light, free movements, now sitting back

upon his heels to hold the cup of boiling water over the blaze by a curiously contrived handle, now rising and going to the saddle pack for some needed article. There was something graceful as well as powerful about his every motion. He gave one a sense of strength and almost infinite resource. Then suddenly her imagination conjured there beside him the man from whom she had fled, and in the light of this fine face the other face darkened and weakened and she had a swift revelation of his true character, and wondered that she had never known before. A shudder passed over her, and a gray pallor came into her face at the memory. She felt a great distaste for thinking of the necessity for even living at that moment.

Then at once he was beside her with a tin plate and the cup of steaming tea, and began to feed her, as if she had been a baby, roast rabbit and toasted corn bread. She ate unquestioningly, and drank her tea, finding all delicious after her long fast, and gaining new strength with every mouthful.

"How did I get here?" she asked suddenly; rising to one elbow and looking around. "I don't seem to remember a place like this."

"I found you hanging on a bush in the moonlight," he said gravely, "and brought you here."

Hazel lay back and reflected on this. He had brought her here. Then he must have carried her! Well, his arms looked strong enough to lift a heavier person than herself—but he had brought her here!

A faint colour stole into her pale cheeks.

"Thank you," she said at last. "I suppose I wasn't just able to come myself." There was a droll little pucker at the corner of her mouth.

"Not exactly," he answered as he gathered up the dishes.

"I remember that crazy little steed of mine began to climb straight up the side of a terrible wall in the dark, and finally decided to wipe me off with a tree. That is the last I can recall. I felt myself slipping and couldn't hold on any longer. Then it all got dark and I let go."

"Where were you going?" asked the young man.

"Going? I wasn't going anywhere," said the girl; "the pony was doing that. He was running away, I suppose. He ran miles and hours with me and I couldn't stop him. I lost hold on the bridle, you see, and he had ideas about what he wanted to do. I was almost frightened to death, and there wasn't a soul in sight all day. I never saw such an empty place in my life. It can't be this is still Arizona, we came so far.''

"When did you start?'' the missionary questioned gravely.

"Why, this morning,—that is—why, it must have been yesterday. I'm sure I don't know when. It was Wednesday morning about eleven o'clock that we left the car on horse-back to visit a mine papa had heard about. It seems about a year since we started.''

"How many were in your party?'' asked the young man.

"Just papa and my brother, and Mr. Hamar, a friend of my father's,'' answered the girl, her cheeks reddening at the memory of the name.

"But was there no guide, no native with you at all?'' There was anxiety in the young man's tone. He had visions of other lost people who would have to be looked after.

"Oh, yes, there was the man my father had written to, who brought the horses, and two or three men with him, some of them Indians, I think. His name was Bunce, Mr. Bunce. He was a queer man with a lot of wild looking hair.''

"Shag Bunce,'' said the missionary thoughtfully. "But if Shag was along I cannot understand how you came to get so widely separated from your party. He rides the fastest horse in this region. No pony of his outfit, be he ever so fleet, could get far ahead of Shag Bunce. He would have caught you within a few minutes. What happened? Was there an accident?''

He looked at her keenly, feeling sure there was some mystery behind her wanderings that he ought to unravel for the sake of the girl and her friends. Hazel's cheeks grew rosy.

"Why, nothing really happened,'' she said evasively. "Mr. Bunce was ahead with my father. In fact he was out of sight when my pony started to run. I was riding with Mr. Hamar, and as we didn't care anything about the mine we didn't hurry. Before we realized it the others were far ahead over a hill or something, I forget what was ahead, only they couldn't be seen. Then we—I—that is—well, I must have touched my pony pretty hard with my whip and he wheeled and started to run. I'm not sure but I touched Mr. Hamar's horse, too, and he was behaving badly. I really hadn't time to see. I don't know what became of Mr. Hamar. He isn't much of a horseman. I don't believe he had ever ridden before. He may have had some trouble with his horse. Anyway before I knew it I was out of sight of everything but wide empty stretches with mountains and clouds at the end everywhere, and going on and on and not getting any nearer to anything.''

"This Mr. Hamar must have been a fool not to have given an alarm to your friends at once if he could do nothing himself," said Brownleigh sternly. "I cannot understand how it could happen that no one found you sooner. It was the merest chance that I came upon your whip and other little things and so grew anxious lest some one was lost. It is very strange that no one found you before this. Your father will have been very anxious.''

Hazel sat up with flaming cheeks and began to gather her hair in a knot. A sudden realization of her position had come upon her and given her strength.

"Well, you see," she stumbled, trying to explain without telling anything, "Mr. Hamar might have thought I had gone back to the car, or he might have thought I would turn back in a few minutes. I do not think he would have wanted to follow me just then. I was—angry with him!''

The young missionary looked at the beautiful girl sitting upright on the canvas he had spread for her bed, trying vainly to reduce her bright hair to something like order, her cheeks glowing, her eyes shining now, half with anger, half with embarrassment, and for a second he pitied the one who had incurred her wrath. A strange unreasoning anger towards the unknown man took possession of him, and his face grew tender as he watched the girl.

"That was no excuse for letting you go alone into the perils of the desert," he said severly. "He could not have known. It was impossible that he could have understood or he would have risked his life to save you from what you have been through. No man could do otherwise!''

Hazel looked up, surprised at the vehemence of the words, and again the contrast between the two men struck her forcibly.

"I am afraid," she murmured looking off towards the distant mountains thoughtfully, "that he isn't much of a man.''

And somehow the young missionary was relieved to hear

her say so. There was a moment's embarrassed silence and then Brownleigh began to search in his pocket, as he saw the golden coil of hair beginning to slip loose from its knot again.

"Will these help you any?" he asked handing out the comb and hairpins he had found a sudden awkwardness coming upon him.

"Oh, my own comb!" she exclaimed. "And hairpins! Where did you find them? Indeed they will help," and she seized upon them eagerly.

He turned away embarrassed, marvelling at the touch of her fingers as she took the bits of shell from his hand. No woman's hand like that had touched his own, even in greeting, since he bade good-bye to his invalid mother and came out to these wilds to do his work. It thrilled him to the very soul and he was minded of the sweet awe that had come upon him in his own cabin as he looked upon the little articles of woman's toilet lying upon his table as if they were at home. He could not understand his own mood. It seemed like weakness. He turned aside and frowned at himself for his foolish sentimentality towards a stranger whom he had found upon the desert. He laid it to the weariness of the long journey and the sleepless night.

"I found them in the sand. They showed me the way to find you," he said, trying vainly to speak in a commonplace tone. But somehow his voice seemed to take on a deep significance. He looked at her shyly, half fearing she must feel it, and then murmuring something about looking after the horses he hurried away.

When he came back she had mastered the rebellious hair, and it lay shining and beautiful, braided and coiled about her shapely head. She was standing now, having shaken down and smoothed out the rumpled riding habit, and had made herself look quite fresh and lovely in spite of the limited toilet conveniences.

He caught his breath as he saw her. The two regarded one another intensely for just an instant, each startlingly conscious of the other's personality, as men and women will sometimes get a glimpse beyond mere body and sight the soul. Each was aware of a thrilling pleasure in the presence of the other. It was something new and wonderful that could not be expressed nor even put into thoughts as yet but something none the less real that flashed along their consciousness like the song of the native bird, the scent of the violet, the breath of the morning.

The instant of soul recognition passed and then each recovered self-possession, but it was the woman who spoke first.

"I feel very much more respectable," she laughed pleasantly. "Where is my vicious little horse? Isn't it time we were getting back?"

Then a cloud of anxiety came over the brightness of the man's face.

"That is what I was coming to tell you," he said in a troubled tone. "The wicked little beast has eaten off his hobble and fled. There isn't a sight of him to be seen far or wide. He must have cleared out while we were at dinner, for he was munching grass peaceably enough before you woke up. It was careless of me not to make him more secure. The hobble was an old one and worn, but the best I had. I came back to tell you that I must ride after him at once. You won't be afraid to stay alone for a little while, will you? My horse has had a rest. I think I ought to be able to catch him."

V

The Trail

But the look of horror in the eyes of the girl stopped him.

She gave a quick frightened glance around and then her eyes besought him. All the terror of the night alone in the wideness returned upon her. She heard again the howl of the coyotes, and saw the long dark shadows in the canyon. She was white to the lips with the thought of it.

"Oh, don't leave me alone!" she said trying to speak bravely. "I don't feel as if I could stand it. There are wild beasts around"—she glanced furtively behind her as if even now one was slyly tracking her—"it was awful—awful! Their howls! And it is so alone here!—I never was alone before!"

There was that in her appealing helplessness that gave him a wild desire to stoop and fold her in his arms and tell her he would never leave her while she wanted him. The colour came and went in his fine bronzed face, and his eyes grew tender with feeling.

"I won't leave you," he said gently, "not if you feel that way, though there is really no danger here in daytime. The wild creatures are very shy and only show themselves at night. But if I do not find your horse how are you to get speedily back to your friends? It is a long distance you have come, and you could not ride alone."

Her face grew troubled.

"Couldn't I walk?" she suggested. "I'm a good walker. I've walked five miles at once many a time."

"We are at least forty miles from the railroad," he smiled back at her, "and the road is rough, over a mountain by the nearest way. Your horse must have been determined indeed to take you so far in one day. He is evidently a new purchase of Shag's and bent on returning to his native heath. Horses do that sometimes. It is their instinct. I'll tell you what I'll do. It may be that he has only gone down in the valley to the water-hole. There is one not far away, I think. I'll go to the edge of the mesa and get a view. If he is not far away you can come with me after him. Just sit here and watch me. I'll not go out of your sight or hearing, and I'll not be gone five minutes. You'll not be afraid?''

She sat down obediently where he bade her, her eyes large with fear, for she dreaded the loneliness of the desert more than any fear that had ever visited her before.

''I promise I'll not go beyond your sight and call,'' he reassured her and with a smile turned towards his own horse, and swinging himself into the saddle galloped rapidly away to the edge of the mesa.

She watched him riding away, her fears almost forgotten in her admiration of him, her heart beating strangely with the memory of his smile. The protection of it seemed to linger behind him, and quiet her anxiety.

He rode straight to the east, and then more slowly turned and skirted the horizon, riding north along the edge of the mesa. She saw him shade his eyes with his hand and look away in all directions. At last after a prolonged gaze straight north he wheeled his horse and came quickly back to her.

His face was grave as he dismounted.

''I've sighted him,'' he said, ''but it's no use. He has three or four miles start, and a steep hill climbed. When he reaches the top of the next mesa he has a straight course before him, and probably down-hill after that. It might take me three or four hours to catch him and it's a question if I could do it then. We'll have to dismiss him from our arrangements and get along with Billy. Do you feel equal to riding now? Or ought you to rest again?''

''Oh, I can ride, but—I cannot take your horse. What will you do?''

''I shall do nicely,'' he answered smiling again; ''only our progress will be slower than if we had both horses. What a pity that I had not taken off his saddle! It would have been more comfortable for you than this. But I was searching so anxiously for the rider that I took little heed to the horse except to hastily hobble him. And when I found you you needed all my attention. Now I advise you to lie down and rest until I get packed up. It won't take me long.''

She curled down obediently to rest until he was ready to fold up the canvas on which she lay, and watched his easy movements as he put together the few articles of the pack, and arranged the saddle for her comfort. Then he strode over to her.

"With your permission," he said and stooping picked her up lightly in his arms and placed her on the horse.

"I beg your pardon," he said, "but you are not equal to the exertion of mounting in the ordinary way. You will need every bit of strength for the ride. You are weaker than you realize."

Her laugh rippled out faintly.

"You make me feel like an insignificant baby. I didn't know what was happening until you had me here. You must have the strength of a giant. I never felt so little before."

"You are not a heavy burden," he said smiling. "Now are you quite comfortable? If so we'll start."

Billy arched his neck and turned his head proudly to survey his new rider, a look of friendliness on his bay face and in his kindly eye.

"Oh, isn't he a beauty!" exclaimed the girl reaching out a timid hand to pat his neck. The horse bowed and almost seemed to smile. Brownleigh noticed the gleam of a splendid jewel on the little hand.

"Billy is my good friend and constant companion," said the missionary. "We've faced some long, hard days together. He is wanting me to tell you now that he is proud to carry you back to your friends."

Billy bowed up and down and smiled again, and Hazel laughed out with pleasure. Then her face grew sober again.

"But you will have to walk," she said. "I cannot take your horse and let you walk. I won't do that. I'm going to walk with you."

"And use up what strength you have so that you could not even ride?" he said pleasantly. "No, I couldn't allow that, you know, and I am pleased to walk with a companion. A missionary's life is pretty lonesome sometimes, you know. Come, Billy, we must be starting, for we want to make a good ten miles before we stop to rest if our guest can stand the journey."

With stately steppings as if he knew he bore a princess

Billy started; and with long, easy strides Brownleigh walked by his side, ever watchful of the way, and furtively observing the face of the girl, whose strength he well knew must be extremely limited after her ride of the day before.

Out on the top of the mesa looking off towards the great mountains and the wide expanse of seemingly infinite shades and colourings Hazel drew her breath in wonder at the beauty of the scene. Her companion called her attention to this and that point of interest. The slender dark line across the plain was mesquite. He told her how when once they had entered it it would seem to spread out vastly as though it filled the whole valley, and that then looking back the grass slope below them would seem to be an insignificant streak of yellow. He told her it was always so in this land, that the kind of landscape through which one was passing filled the whole view and seemed the only thing in life. He said he supposed it was so in all our lives, that the immediate present filled the whole view of the future until we came to something else; and the look in his eyes made her turn from the landscape and wonder about him and his life.

Then he stooped and pointed to a clump of soapweed, and idly broke off a bit of another bush, handing it to her.

"The Indians call it 'the weed that was not scared,' " he said. "Isn't it an odd suggestive name?"

"It must be a brave little weed indeed to live out here all alone under this terribly big sky. I wouldn't like it even if I were only a weed," and she looked around and shivered with the thought of her fearful ride alone in the night. But she tucked the little spray of brave green into the buttonhole of her riding habit and it looked of prouder lineage than any weed as it rested against the handsome darkness of the rich green cloth. For an instant the missionary studied the picture of the lovely girl on the horse and forgot that he was only a missionary. Then with a start he came to himself. They must be getting on, for the sun had already passed its zenith, and the way was long before them. His eyes lingered wistfully on the gleam of her hair where the sun touched it into burnished gold. Then he remembered.

"By the way, is this yours?" he asked and brought out of his pocket the little velvet cap.

"Oh, where did you find it?" she cried, settling it on her

head like a touch of velvet in a crown. "I dropped it in front of a tiny little cabin when my last hope vanished. I called and called but the wind threw my voice back into my throat and no one came out to answer me."

"It was my house," he said. "I found it on a sage-bush a few feet from my own door. Would that I had been at home to answer your call!"

"Your house!" she exclaimed, in wonder. "Oh, why, it couldn't have been. It wasn't big enough for anybody—not anybody like you—to live in. Why, it wasn't anything more than a—a shed,—just a little board shanty."

"Exactly; my shack!" he said half apologetically, half comically. "You should see the inside. It's not so bad as it looks. I only wish I could take you that way, but the fact is it's somewhat out of the way to the railroad, and we must take the short cut if we want to shorten your father's anxiety. Do you feel able to go on further now?"

"Oh, yes, quite," she said with sudden trouble in her face. "Papa will be very much worried, and Aunt Maria—oh, Aunt Maria will be wild with anxiety. She will tell me that this is just what she expected from my going out riding in this heathen land. She warned me not to go. She said it wasn't ladylike."

As they went on gradually she told him all about her people, describing their little idiosyncrasies; her aunt, her brother, her father, her maid and even the fat man cook. The young man soon had the picture of the private car with all its luxuries, and the story of the days of travel that had been one long fairy tale of pleasure. Only the man Hamar was not mentioned; but the missionary had forgotten him. Somehow he had taken a dislike to him from the first mention of his name. He blamed him fiercely for not having come after the maiden, yet blessed the fortune that had given himself that honour.

They were descending into the canyon now, but not by the steep trail up which the pony had taken her the night before. However it was rough enough and the descent, though it was into the very heart of nature's beauty storehouse, yet frightened Hazel. She started at every steep place, and clutched at the saddle wildly, pressing her white teeth hard into her under lip until it grew white and tense. Her face was white also, and a sudden faintness seemed to come upon her. Brownleigh noticed instantly, and walking close beside the horse, guiding carefully his every step, he put his free arm about her to steady her, and bade her lean towards him and not be afraid.

His strength steadied her and gave her confidence; and his pleasant voice pointing out the beauties of the way helped her to forget her fright. He made her look up and showed her how the great ferns were hanging over the fringe of green at the top of the bare rocks above, their delicate lacery standing out like green fretwork against the blue of the sky. He pointed to a cave in the rocks far above, and told her of the dwellers of old who had hollowed it out for a home; of the stone axes and jars of clay, the corn mills and sandals woven of yucca that were found there; and of other curious cave-houses in this part of the country; giving in answer to her wondering questions much curious information, the like of which she had never heard before.

Then when they were fairly down in the shadows of the canyon he brought her a cooling draught of spring water in the tin cup, and lifting her unexpectedly from the horse made her sit in a mossy spot where sweet flowers clustered about, and rest for a few minutes, for he knew the ride down the steep path had been terribly trying to her nerves.

Yet all his attentions to her, whether lifting her to and from the saddle, or putting his arm about her to support her on the way, were performed with such grace of courtesy as to remove all personality from his touch, and she marvelled at it while she sat and rested and watched him from the distance watering Billy at a noisy little stream that chattered through the canyon.

He put her on the horse again and they took their way through the coolness and beauty of the canyon winding along the edge of the little stream, threading their way among the trees, and over boulders and rough places until at last in the late afternoon they came out again upon the plain.

The missionary looked anxiously at the sun. It had taken longer to come through the canyon than he had anticipated. The day was waning. He quickened Billy into a trot and settled into a long athletic run beside him, while the girl's cheeks flushed with the exercise and wind, and her admiration of her escort grew.

"But aren't you very tired?" she asked at last when he slowed down and made Billy walk again. Billy, by the way, had enjoyed the race immensely. He thought he was having a grand time with a princess on his back and his beloved master keeping pace with him. He was confident by this time that they were bringing the princess home to be there to welcome them on all returns hereafter. His horse-sense had jumped to a conclusion and approved most heartily.

"Tired!" answered Brownleigh and laughed; "not consiously. I'm good for several miles yet myself. I haven't had such a good time in three years, not since I left home—and mother," he added softly, reverently.

There was a look in his eyes that made the girl long to know more. She watched him keenly and asked:

"Oh, then you have a mother!"

"Yes, I have a mother,—a wonderful mother!" He breathed the words like a blessing. The girl looked at him in awe. She had no mother. Her own had died before she could remember. Aunt Maria was her only idea of mothers.

"Is she out here?" she asked.

"No, she is at home up in New Hampshire in a little quiet country town, but she is a wonderful mother."

"And have you no one else, no other family out here with you?"

Hazel did not realize how anxiously she awaited the answer to that question. Somehow she felt a jealous dislike of any one who might belong to him, even a mother—and a sudden thought of sister or wife who might share the little shanty cabin with him made her watch his face narrowly. But the answer was quick, with almost a shadow like deep longing on his face:

"Oh, no, I have no one. I'm all alone. And sometimes if it were not for mother's letters it would seem a great way from home."

The girl did not know why it was so pleasant to know this, and why her heart went out in instant sympathy for him.

"O-oo!" she said gently. "Tell me about your mother, please!"

And so he told her, as he walked beside her, of his invalid mother whose frail body and its needs bound her to a couch in her old New England home, helpless and carefully tended

48

by a devoted nurse whom she loved and who loved her. Her great spirit had risen to the sacrifice of sending her only son out to the desert on his chosen commission.

They had been climbing a long sloping hill, and at the climax of the story had reached the top and could look abroad again over a wide expanse of country. It seemed to Hazel's city bred eyes as though the kingdoms of the whole world lay spread before her awed gaze. A brilliant sunset was spreading a great silver light behind the purple mountains in the west, red and blue in flaming lavishness, with billows of white clouds floating above, and over that in sharp contrast the sky was velvet black with storm. To the south the rain was falling in a brilliant shower like yellow gold, and to the east two more patches of rain were rosy pink as petals of some wondrous flowers, and arching over them a half rainbow. Turning slightly towards the north one saw the rain falling from dark blue clouds in great streaks of white light.

"Oh-oo!" breathed the girl; "how wonderful! I never saw anything like that before."

But the missionary had no time for answer. He began quickly to unstrap the canvas from behind the saddle, watching the clouds as he did so.

"We are going to get a wetting, I'm afraid," he said and looked anxiously at his companion.

VI

Camp

It came indeed before he was quite ready for it, but he managed to throw the canvas over horse and lady, bidding her hold it on one side while he, standing close under the extemporized tent, held the other side, leaving an opening in front for air, and so they managed to keep tolerably dry, while two storms met overhead and poured down a torrent upon them.

The girl laughed out merrily as the first great splashes struck her face, then retreated into the shelter as she was bidden and sat quietly watching, and wondering over it all.

Here was she, a carefully nurtured daughter of society, until now never daring to step one inch beyond the line of conventionality, sitting afar from all her friends and kindred on a wide desert plain, under a bit of canvas with a strange missionary's arm about her, and sitting as securely and contentedly, nay happily, as if she had been in her own cushioned chair in her New York boudoir. It is true the arm was about her for the purpose of holding down the canvas and keeping out the rain, but there was a wonderful security and sense of strength in it that filled her with a strange new joy and made her wish that the elements of the universe might continue to rage in brilliant display about her head a little longer, if thereby she might continue to feel the strength of that fine presence near her and about her. A great weariness was upon her and this was rest and content, so she put all other thoughts out of her mind for the time and rested back against the strong arm in full realization of her safety amidst the disturbance of the elements.

The missionary wore his upward look. No word passed between them as the panorama of the storm swept by. Only God knew what was passing in his soul, and how out of that dear nearness of the beautiful girl a great longing was born to have her always near him, his right to ever protect her from the storms of life.

But he was a man of marked self-control. He held even his thoughts in obedience to a higher power, and while the wild wish of his heart swept exquisitely over him he stood calmly, and handed it back to heaven, as though he knew it were a wandering wish, a testing of his true self.

At the first instant of relief from necessity he took his arm away. He did not presume a single second to hold the canvas after the wind had subsided, and she liked him the better for it, and felt her trust in him grow deeper as he gently shook the raindrops from their temporary shelter.

The rain had lasted but a few minutes, and as the clouds cleared the earth grew lighter for a space. Gently melting into the silver and amethyst and emerald of the sky the rainbow faded and now they hurried on, for Brownleigh wished to reach a certain spot where he hoped to find dry shelter for the night. He saw that the excitement of travel and the storm had sorely spent the strength of the girl, and that she needed rest, so he urged the horse forward, and hurried along by his side.

But suddenly he halted the horse and looked keenly into the face of his companion in the dying light.

"You are very tired," he said. "You can hardly sit up any longer."

She smiled faintly.

Her whole body was drooping with weariness and a strange sick faintness had come upon her.

"We must stop here," he said and cast about him for a suitable spot. "Well, this will do. Here is a dry place, the shelter of that big rock. The rain was from the other direction, and the ground around here did not even get sprinkled. That group of trees will do for a private room for you. We'll soon have a fire and some supper and then you'll feel better."

With that he stripped off his coat and, spreading it upon the ground in the dry shelter of a great rock, lifted the drooping girl from the saddle and laid her gently on the coat.

She closed her eyes wearily and sank back. In truth she was nearer to fainting than she had ever been in her life, and the young man hastened to administer a restorative which brought the colour back to her pale cheeks.

"It is nothing," she murmured, opening her eyes and trying to smile. "I was just tired, and my back ached with so much riding."

"Don't talk!" he said gently. "I'll give you something to hearten you up in a minute."

He quickly gathered sticks and soon had a blazing fire not far from where she lay, and the glow of it played over her face and her golden hair, while he prepared a second cup of beef extract, and blessed the fortune that had made him fill his canteen with water at the spring in the canyon, for water might not be very near, and he felt that to have to move the girl further along that night would be a disaster. He could see that she was about used up. But while he was making preparations for supper, Billy, who was hobbled but entirely able to edge about slowly, had discovered a water-hole for himself, and settled that difficulty. Brownleigh drew a sigh of relief, and smiled happily as he saw his patient revive under the influence of the hot drink and a few minutes' rest.

"I'm quite able to go on a little further," she said, sitting up with an effort, "if you think we should go further tonight. I really don't feel bad at all any more."

He smiled with relief.

"I'm so glad," he said; "I was afraid I had made you travel too far. No, we'll not go further till daylight, I think. This is as good a place to camp as any, and water not far away. You will find your boudoir just inside that group of trees, and in half an hour or so the canvas will be quite dry for your bed. I've got it spread out, you see, close to the fire on the other side there. And it wasn't wet through. The blanket was sheltered. It will be warm and dry. I think we can make you comfortable. Have you ever slept out under the stars before—that is, of course, with the exception of last night? I don't suppose you really enjoyed that experience."

Hazel shuddered at the thought.

"I don't remember much only awful darkness and howling. Will those creatures come this way, do you think? I feel as if I should die with fright if I have to hear them again."

"You may hear them in the distance, but not nearby," he answered reassuringly; "they do not like the fire. They will not come near nor disturb you. Besides, I shall be close at

52

hand all night. I am used to listening and waking in the night. I shall keep a bright fire blazing."

"But you—you—what will you do? You are planning to give me the canvas and the blanket, and stay awake yourself keeping watch. You have walked all day while I have ridden, and you have been nurse and cook as well, while I have been good for nothing. And now you want me to rest comfortably all night while you sit up."

There was a ring in the young man's voice as he answered her that thrilled her to the heart.

"I shall be all right," he said, and his voice was positively joyous, "and I shall have the greatest night of my life taking care of you. I count it a privilege. Many a night have I slept alone under the stars with no one to guard, and felt the loneliness. Now I shall always have this to remember. Besides, I shall not sit up. I am used to throwing myself down anywhere. My clothing is warm, and my saddle is used to acting as a pillow. I shall sleep and rest, and yet be always on the alert to keep up the fire and hear any sound that comes near." He talked as though he were recounting the plan of some delightful recreation, and the girl lay and watched his handsome face in the play of the firelight and rejoiced in it. Somehow there was something very sweet in companionship alone in the vast silence with this stranger friend. She found herself glad of the wideness of the desert and the stillness of the night that shut out the world and made their most unusual relationship possible for a little while. A great longing possessed her to know more and understand better the fine personality of this man who was a man among men, she was convinced.

Suddenly as he came and sat down by the fire not far from her after attending to the few supper dishes, she burst forth with a question:

"Why did you do it?"

He turned to her eyes that were filled with a deep content and asked, "Do what?"

"Come here! Be a missionary! Why did you do it? You are fitted for better things. You could fill a large city church, or—even do other things in the world. Why did you do it?"

The firelight flickered on his face and showed his features fine and strong in an expression of deep feeling that gave it an exalted look. There seemed a light in his eyes that was more than firelight as he raised them upward in a swift glance and said quietly, as though it were the simplest matter in the universe:

"Because my Father called me to this work. And—I doubt if there can be any better. Listen!"

And then he told her of his work while the fire burned cheerfully, and the dusk grew deeper, till the moon showed clear her silver orb riding high in starry heavens.

The mournful voice of the coyotes echoed distantly, but the girl was not frightened, for her thoughts were held by the story of the strange childlike race for whom this man among men was giving his life.

He told her of the Indian hogans, little round huts built of logs on end, and slanting to a common centre thatched with turf and straw, an opening for a door and another in the top to let out the smoke of the fire, a dirt floor, no furniture but a few blankets, sheepskins, and some tin dishes. He carried her in imagination to one such hogan where lay the little dying Indian maiden and made the picture of their barren lives so vivid that tears stood in her eyes as she listened. He told of the medicine-men, the ignorance and superstition, the snake dances and heathen rites; the wild, poetic, conservative man of the desert with his distrust, his great loving heart, his broken hopes and blind aspirations: until Hazel began to see that he really loved them, that he had seen the possibility of greatness in them, and longed to help develop it.

He told her of the Sabbath just past, when in company with his distant neighbour missionary he had gone on an evangelistic tour among the tribes far away from the mission station. He pictured the Indians sitting on rocks and stones amid the long shadows of the cedar trees, just before the sundown, listening to a sermon. He had reminded them of their Indian god Begochiddi and of Nilhchii whom the Indians believe to have made all things, the same whom white men call God; and showed them a book called the Bible which told the story of God, and of Jesus His Son who came to save men from their sin. Not one of the Indians had ever heard the name of Jesus before, nor knew anything of the great story of salvation.

Hazel found herself wondering why it made so very much difference whether these poor ignorant creatures knew all this or not, and yet she saw from the face of the man before her that it did matter, infinitely. To him it mattered more than anything else. A passing wish that she were an Indian to thus hold his interest flashed through her mind, but he was speaking yet of his work, and his rapt look filled her with awe. She was overwhelmed with the greatness and the fineness of the man before her. Sitting there in the fitful firelight, with its ruddy glow upon his face, his fat off and the moon laying a silver crown upon his head, he seemed half angel, half god. She had never before been so filled with the joy of beholding another soul. She had no room for thoughts of anything else.

Then suddenly he remembered that it was late.

"I have kept you awake far too long," he said penitently, looking at her with a smile that seemed all tenderness. "We ought to get on our way as soon as it is light, and I have made you listen to me when you ought to have been sleeping. But I always like to have a word with my Father before retiring. Shall we have our worship together?"

Hazel, overcome by wonder and embarrassment, assented and lay still in her sheltered spot watching him as he drew a small leather book from his breast pocket and opened to the place marked by a tiny silken cord. Then stirring up the fire to brightness he began to read and the majestic words of the ninety-first psalm came to her unaccustomed ears as a charmed page.

"He that dwelleth in the secret place of the Most High shall abide under the shadow of the Almighty."

"He shall cover thee with His feathers and under His wings shalt thou trust." The words were uttered with a ringing tone of trust. The listener knew little of birds and their ways, but the phrasing reminded her of the way she had been sheltered from the storm a little while before and her heart thrilled anew with the thought of it.

"Thou shalt not be afraid for the terror by night!"

Ah! Terror by night! She knew what that meant. That awful night of darkness, steep riding, howling beasts and black oblivion! She shuddered involuntarily at the remembrance. Not afraid! What confidence the voice had as it rang on, and all at once she knew that this night was free from terror for her because of the man whose confidence was in the Unseen.

"He shall give His angels charge over thee," and looking at him she half expected to see flitting wings in the moonlit background. How strong and true the face! How tender the lines about the mouth! What a glow of inner quietness and power in the eyes as he raised them now and again to her face across the firelight! What a thing it would be to have a friend like that always to guard one! Her eyes glowed softly at the thought and once again there flashed across her mind the contrast between this man and the one from whom she had fled in horror the day before.

The reading ended, he replaced the little marker, and dropping upon one knee on the desert with his face lifted to the sky and all the radiance of the moon flooding over him he spoke to God as a man speaks with his friend, face to face.

Hazel lay with open, wondering eyes and watched him, awe growing within her. The sense of an unseen Presence close at hand was so strong that once she lifted half frightened eyes to the wide clear sky. The light on the face of the missionary seemed like glory from another world.

She felt herself enfolded and upborne into the Presence of the infinite by his words, and he did not forget to commend her loved ones to the care of the Almighty. A great peace came upon her as she listened to the simple, earnest words and a sense of security such as she had never known before.

After the brief prayer he turned to her with a smile and a few words of assurance about the night. There was her dressing-room behind those trees, and she need not be afraid; he would not be far away. He would keep the fire bright all night so that she would not be annoyed by the near howling of the coyotes. Then he moved away to gather more wood, and she heard him singing, softly at first, and then gathering volume as he got further away, his rich tenor voice ringing clear upon the night in an old hymn. The words floated back distinctly to her listening ears:

> "My God, is any hour so sweet
>   From flush of dawn to evening star,
>   As that which calls me to Thy feet,
>   The hour of prayer?

"Then is my strength by Thee renewed;
  Then are my sins by Thee forgiven;
  Then dost Thou cheer my solitude
    With hopes of heaven.

"No words can tell what sweet relief
  There for my every want I find;
  What strength for warfare, balm for grief,
    What peace of mind!"

She lay down for the night marvelling still over the man. He was singing those words as if he meant every one, and she knew that he possessed something that made him different from other men. What was it? It seemed to her that he was the one man of all the earth, and how was it that she had found him away out here alone in the desert?

The great stars burned sharply in the heavens over her, the white radiance of the moon lay all about her, the firelight played at her feet. Far away she could hear the howling of the coyotes, but she was not afraid.

She could see the broad shoulders of the man as he stooped over on the other side of the fire to throw on more wood. Presently she knew he had thrown himself down with his head on the saddle, but she could hear him still humming softly something that sounded like a lullaby. When the firelight flared up it showed his fine profile.

Not far away she could hear Billy cropping the grass, and throughout the vast open universe there seemed to brood a great and peaceful silence. She was very tired and her eyelids drooped shut. The last thing she remembered was a line he had read from the little book, "He shall give His angels charge——" and she wondered if they were somewhere about now.

That was all until she awoke suddenly with the consciousness that she was alone, and that in the near distance a conversation in a low tone was being carried on.

VII

Revelation

The moon was gone, and the luminous silver atmosphere was turned into a clear dark blue, with shadows of the blackness of velvet; but the stars burned redder now, and nearer to the earth.

The fire still flickered brightly, with a glow the moon had paled before she went to sleep, but there was no protecting figure on the other side of the flames, and the angels seemed all to have forgotten.

Off at a little distance, where a group of sage-brush made dense darkness, she heard the talking. One speaking in low tones, now pleading, now explaining, deeply earnest, with a mingling of anxiety and trouble. She could not hear any words. She seemed to know the voice was low that she might not hear; yet it filled her with a great fear. What had happened? Had some one come to harm them, and was he pleading for her life? Strange to say it never entered her head to doubt his loyalty, stranger though he was. Her only feeling was that he might have been overpowered in his sleep, and be even now in need of help himself. What could she do?

After the first instant of frozen horror she was on the alert. He had saved her, she must help him. She could not hear any other voice than his. Probably the enemy spoke in whispers, but she knew that she must go at once and find out what was the matter. The distance from her pleasant couch beside the fire was but a few steps, yet it seemed to her frightened heart and trembling limbs, as she crept softly over towards the sage-brush, that it was miles.

At last she was close to the bush, could part it with her cold hand and look into the little shelter.

There was a faint light in the east beyond the mountains that showed the coming dawn, and silhouetted against this she saw the figure of her rescuer, dropped upon one knee, his elbow on the other and his face bowed in his hand. She could hear his words distinctly now, but there was no man else present, though she searched the darkness carefully.

"I found her lost out here in the wilderness," he was saying in low, earnest tones, "so beautiful, so dear! But I know she cannot be for me. Her life has been all luxury and I would not be a man to ask her to share the desert! I know too that she is not fitted for the work. I know it would be all wrong, and I must not wish it, but I love her, though I may not tell her so! I must be resolute and strong, and not show her what I feel. I must face my Gethsemane, for this girl is as dear to me as my own soul! God bless and guard her, for I may not."

The girl had stood rooted to the spot unable to move as the 'ow voice went on with its revelation, but when the plea for a blessing upon her came with all the mighty longing of a soul who loved absorbingly, it was as if she were unable to bear it, and she turned and fled silently back to her couch, creeping under the canvas, thrilled, frightened, shamed and glad all in one. She closed her eyes and the swift tears of joy came. He loved her! He loved her! How the thought thrilled her. How her own heart leaped up to meet his love. The fact of it was all she could contain for the time and it filled her with an ecstasy such as she had never known before. She opened her eyes to the stars and they shone back a great radiance of joy to her. The quiet darkness of the vast earth all about her seemed suddenly to have become the sweetest spot she had known. She had never thought there could be joy like this.

Gradually she quieted the wild throbbing of her heart and tried to set her thoughts in order. Perhaps she was taking too much for granted. Perhaps he was talking of another girl, some one he had met the day before. But yet it seemed as if there could be no doubt. There would not be two girls lost out in that desert. There could not—and her heart told her that he loved her. Could she trust her heart? Oh, the dearness of it if it were true!

Her face was burning too, with the sweet shame of having heard what was not meant for her ears.

Then came the flash of pain in the joy. He did not intend to tell her. He meant to hide his love—and for her sake! And he was great enough to do so. The man who could sacrifice the things that other men hold dear to come out to the wilderness for the sake of a forgotten, half-savage people, could sacrifice anything for what he considered right. This fact loomed like a wall of adamant across the lovely way that joy had revealed to her. Her heart fell with the thought that he was not to speak of this to her,—and she knew that more than for anything else in life, more than anything she had ever known, she longed to hear him speak those words to her. A half resentment filled her that he had told his secret to Another— what concerned her—and would not let her know.

The heart searching went on, and now she came to the thorn-fact of the whole revelation. There had been another reason besides care for herself why he could not tell her of his love,—why he could not ask her to share his life. She had not been accounted worthy. He had put it in pleasant words and said she was unfitted, but he might as well have made it plain and said how useless she would be in his life.

The tears came now, tears of mortification, for Hazel Radcliffe had never before in all her petted life been accounted unworthy for any position. It was not that she considered at all the possibility of accepting the position that was not to be offered her. Her startled mind had not even reached so far; but her pride was hurt to think that any one should think her unworthy.

Then over the whole tumultuous state of mind would come the memory of his voice throbbing with feeling as he said, "She is dear to me as my own soul," and the joy of it would sweep everything else away.

There was no more sleep to be had for her.

The stars grew pale, and the rose dawn grew in the east. She presently heard her companion return and replenish the fire, stirring about softly among the dishes, and move away again, but she had turned her head away that he might not see her face, and he evidently thought her still sleeping.

So she lay and tried to reason things out; tried to scold herself for thinking his words applied to her; tried to recall her city life and friends, and how utterly alien this man and his work would be to them; tried to think of the new day when she would probably reach her friends again and this new friend would be lost sight of; felt a sharp twinge of pain at the thought; wondered if she could meet Milton Hamar and what they would say to one another, and if any sort of comfortable relations could ever be established between them again; and knew they could not. Once again the great horror rolled over her at thought of his kiss. Then came the startling thought that he had used almost the same words to her that his man of the desert had used about her, and yet how infinitely different! How tender and deep and true, and pure and high his face in contrast to the look she had seen upon that handsome, evil face bent over her! She covered her eyes and shuddered again, and entertained a fleeting wish that she might stay forever here and not return to his hated presence.

Then back like a flood-tide of sunshine would come the thought of the missionary and his love for her, and everything else would be obliterated in the rapture it brought.

And thus on rosy wings the morning dawned, a clean, straight sunrise.

Hazel could hear the missionary stepping softly here and there preparing breakfast, and knew he felt it time to be on the move. She must bestir herself and speak, but her cheeks grew pink over the thought of it. She kept waiting and trying to think how to say good-morning without a look of guilty knowledge in her eyes. Presently she heard him call to Billy and move away in the direction where the horse was eating his breakfast. Then snatching her opportunity she slipped from under the canvas into her green boudoir.

But even here she found evidences of her wise guide's care, for standing in front of the largest cedar were two tin cups of clear water and beside them a small pocket soapcase and a clean folded handkerchief, fine and white. He had done his best to supply her with toilet articles.

Her heart leaped up again at his thoughtfulness. She dashed the water into her glowing face, and buried it in the clean folds of the handkerchief, his handkerchief. How wonderful that it should be so! How had a mere commonplace bit of them become so invested with the currents of life as to give such joyful refreshment with a touch! The wonder of it all was like a miracle. She had not known anything in life could be like that.

The great red cliff across the valley was touched with the

morning sun when she emerged from her green shelter, shyly conscious of the secret that lay unrevealed between them.

Their little camp was still in the shadow. The last star had disappeared as if a hand had turned the lights low with a flash and revealed to the morning.

She stood for an instant in the parting of the cedars, a hand on each side holding back the boughs, looking forth from her retreat; and the man advancing saw her and waited with bared head to do her reverence, a great light of love in his eyes which he knew not was visible, but which blinded the eyes of the watching girl, and made her cheeks grow rosier.

The very air about them seemed charged with an electrical current. The little commonplaces which they spoke sank deep into the heart of each and lingered to bless the future. The glances of their eyes had many meetings and lingered shyly on more intimate ground than the day before, yet each had grown more silent. The tenderness of his voice was like a benediction as he greeted her.

He seated her on the canvas he had arranged freshly beside a bit of green grass, and prepared to serve her like a queen. Indeed she wore a queenly bearing, small and slender though she was, her golden hair shining in the morning, and her eyes bright as the stars that had just been paled by day.

There were fried rabbits cooking in the tiny saucepan and corn bread was toasting before the fire on two sharp sticks. She found to her surprise that she was hungry, and that the breakfast he had prepared seemed a most delicious feast.

She grew secure in her consciousness that he did not know she had guessed his secret, and let the joy of it all flow over her and envelop her. Her laugh rang out musically over the plain, and he watched her hungrily, delightedly, enjoying every minute of the companionship with a kind of double joy because of the barren days that he was sure were to come.

Finally he broke away from the pleasant lingering with an exclamation, for the sun was hastening upward and it was time they were on their way. Hastily he packed away the things, she trying in her bungling unaccustomedness to help and only giving sweet hindrance, with the little white hands that thrilled him so wonderfully as they came near with a plate or a cup, or a bit of corn bread that had been left out.

He put her on the horse and they started on their way. Yet

not once in all the pleasant contact had he betrayed his secret, and Hazel began to feel the burden of what she had found out weighing guiltily upon her like a thing stolen which she would gladly replace but dared not. Sometimes, as they rode along, he quietly talking as the day before, pointing out some object of interest, or telling her some remarkable story of his experiences, she would wonder if she had not been entirely misken; heard wrong, maybe, or made more of the words than she should have done. She grew to feel that he could not have meant her at all. And then turning suddenly she would find his eyes upon her with a light in them so tender, so yearning, that she would droop her own in confusion and feel her heart beating wildly with the pleasure and the pain of it.

About noon they came to a rain-water hole near which were three Indian hogans. Brownleigh explained that he had come this way, a little out of the shortest trail, hoping to get another horse so that they might travel faster and reach the railroad before sundown.

The girl's heart went suddenly heavy as he left her sitting on Billy under a cottonwood tree while he went forward to find out if any one was at home and whether they had a horse to spare. Of course she wanted to find her friends and relieve their anxiety as soon as possible, but there was something in the voice of the young missionary as he spoke of hastening onward that seemed to build a wall between them. The pleasant intercourse of the morning seemed drawing so quickly to a close: the wonderful sympathy and interest between them pushed with a violent hand out of her reach. She felt a choking sensation in her throat as if she would like to put her head down on Billy's rough neck-locks and sob.

She tried to reason with herself. It was but a little over twenty-four hours since she first looked upon this stranger, and yet her heart was bound to him in such a way that she was dreading their separation. How could it be? Such things were not real. People always laughed at sudden love affairs as if they were impossible, but her heart told her that it was not merely hours by which they numbered their acquaintance. The soul of this man had been revealed to her in that brief space of time as another's might not have been in years. She dreaded the ending of this companionship. It would be the end, of course. He had said it, and she knew his words were true. His world was not her world, more the pity! He would never give up his world, and he had said she was unfitted for his. It was all too true—this world of rough, uncouth strangers, and wild emptiness of beauty. But how she longed to have this day with him beside her prolonged indefinitely!

The vision would fade of course when she got back into the world again, and things would assume their normal proportions very likely. But just now she admitted to herself that she did not want to get back. She would be entirely content if she might wander thus with him in the desert for the rest of her natural life.

He came back to her presently accompanied by an Indian boy carrying an iron pot and some fresh mutton. Hazel watched them as they built a fire, arranged the pot full of water to boil, and placed the meat to roast. The missionary was making corn cake which presently was baking in the ashes, and giving forth a savoury odour.

An Indian squaw appeared in the doorway of one of the hogans, her baby strapped to her back, and watched her with great round wondering eyes. Hazel smiled at the little papoose, and it soon dimpled into an answering smile. Then she discovered that the missionary was watching them both, his heart in his eyes, a strange wonderful joy in his face, and her heart-beats quickened. She was pleasing him! It was then as she smiled back at the child of the forest that she discovered an interest of her own in these neglected people of his. She could not know that the little dark-skinned baby whom she had noticed would from this time forth become the special tender object of care from the missionary, just because she had noticed it.

They had a merry meal, though not so intimate as the others had been; for a group of Indian women and children huddled outside the nearest hogan watching their every move with wide staring eyes, and stolid but interested countenances; and the little boy hovered not far away to bring anything they might need. It was all pleasant but Hazel felt impatient of the interruption when their time together was now so short. She was glad when, mounted on Billy again, and her companion on a rough little Indian pony with wicked eyes, they rode away together into the sunshine of the afternoon.

But now it seemed but a breathless space before they

would come into the presence of people, for the two horses made rapid time, and the distances flew past them mile by mile, the girl feeling each moment more shy and embarrassed, and conscious of the words she had overheard in the early morning.

It seemed to her a burden she could not carry away unknown upon her soul and yet how could she let him know.

VIII

Reunuciation

They had entered a strip of silvery sand, about two miles wide, and rode almost in silence, for a singular shyness had settled upon them.

The girl was conscious of his eyes upon her with a kind of tender yearning as if he would impress the image on his mind for the time when she would be with him no more. Each had a curious sense of understanding the other's thoughts, and needing no words. But as they neared a great rustling stretch of corn he looked at her keenly again and spoke:

"You are very tired, I'm sure." It was not a question but she lifted her eyes to deny it, and a flood-tide of sweet colour swept over the cheeks. "I knew it," he said, searching her raised eyes. "We must stop and rest after we have passed through this corn. There is a spot under some trees where you will be sheltered from the sun. This corn lasts only a mile or so more, and after you have rested we will have only a short distance to go"—he caught his breath as though the words hurt him—"our journey is almost over!" They rode in silence through the corn, but when it was passed and they were seated beneath the trees the girl lifted her eyes to him filled with unspeakable things.

"I haven't known how to thank you," she said earnestly, the tears almost in evidence.

"Don't, please!" he said gently. "It has been good to me to be with you. How good you never can know." He paused and then looked keenly at her.

"Did you rest well last night, your first night under the stars? Did you hear the coyotes, or feel at all afraid?"

Her colour fled, and she dropped her glance to Billy's neck, while her heart throbbed painfully.

He saw how disturbed she was.

"You were afraid," he charged gently. "Why didn't you call? I was close at hand all the time. What frightened you?"

"Oh, it was nothing!" she said evasively. "It was only for a minute."

"Tell me, please!" his voice compelled her.

"It was just for a minute," she said again, speaking rapidly and trying to hide her embarrassment. "I woke and thought I heard talking and you were not in sight; but it was not long before you came back with an armful of wood, and I saw it was almost morning."

Her cheeks were rosy, as she lifted her clear eyes to meet his searching gaze and tried to face him steadily, but he looked into the very depths of her soul and saw the truth. She felt her courage going from her, and tried to turn her gaze carelessly away, but could not.

At last he said in a low voice full of feeling:

"You heard me?"

Her eyes, which he had held with his look, wavered, faltered, and drooped. "I was afraid," he said as her silence confirmed his conviction. "I heard some one stirring. I looked and thought I saw you going back to your couch." There was grave self-reproach in his tone, but no reproach for her. Nevertheless her heart burned with shame and her eyes filled with tears. She hid her glowing face in her hands and cried out:

"I am so sorry. I did not mean to be listening. I thought from the tone of your voice you were in trouble. I was afraid some one had attacked you, and perhaps I could do something to help——"

"You poor child!" he said deeply moved. "How unpardonable of me to frighten you. It is my habit of talking aloud when I am alone. The great loneliness out here has cultivated it. I did not realize that I might disturb you. What must you think of me? What *can* you think?"

"Think!" she burst forth softly. "I think you are all wrong to try to keep a thing like that to yourself!"

And then the full meaning of what she had said broke upon her, and her face crimsoned with embarrassment.

But he was looking at her with an eager light in his eyes.

"What do you mean?" he asked. "Won't you please explain?"

Hazel was sitting now with her face entirely turned away, and the soft hair blowing concealingly about her burning cheeks. She felt as if she must get up and run away into the desert and end this terrible conversation. She was getting in deeper and deeper every minute.

"Please!" said the gentle, firm voice.

"Why, I—think—a—a—woman—has a right—to know—a thing like that!" she faltered desperately.

"Why?" asked the voice again after a pause.

"Because—she—she—might not ever—she might not ever know there was such a love for a woman in the world!" she stammered, still with her head turned quite away from him. She felt that she could never turn around and face this wonderful man of the desert again. She wished the ground would open and show her some comfortable way of escape.

The pause this time was long, so long that it frightened her, but she dared not turn and look at him. If she had done so she would have seen that he was sitting with bowed head for some time, in deep meditation, and that at last he lifted his glance to the sky again as if to ask a swift permission. Then he spoke.

"A man has no right to tell a woman he loves her when he cannot ask her to marry him."

"That," said the girl, her throat throbbing painfully, "*that* has nothing to do with it. I—was—not talking about—marrying! But I think she has a right to know. It would—make a difference all her life!" Her throat was dry and throbbing. The words seemed to stick as she tried to utter them, yet they would be said. She longed to hide her burning face in some cool shelter and get away from this terrible talk; but she could only sit rigidly quiet, her fingers fastened tensely in the coarse grass at her side.

There was a longer silence now, and still she dared not look at the man.

A great eagle appeared in the heaven above and sailed swiftly and strongly towards a mountain peak. Hazel had a sense of her own smallness, and of the fact that her words had made an exquisite anguish for the soul of her companion, yet she could not think of anything to say that would better matters. At last he spoke, and his voice was like one performing a sad and sacred rite for one tenderly beloved:

"And now that you know I love you can it possibly make any difference to you?"

Hazel tried three times to answer, but every time her trembling lips would frame no words. Then suddenly her face went into her hands and the tears came. She felt as if a benediction had been laid upon her head, and the glory of it was greater than she could bear.

The man watched her, his arms longing to enfold her and soothe her agitation, but he would not. His heart was on fire with the sweetness and the pain of the present moment, yet he could not take advantage of their situation upon the lonely plain, and desecrate the beauty of the trust she had put upon him.

Then her strength came again, and she raised her head and looked into his waiting eyes with a trembling, shy glance, yet true and earnest.

"It will make a difference—to me!" she said. "I shall never feel quite the same towards life again because I know there is such a wonderful man in the world."

She had fine control of her voice now, and was holding back the tears. Her manner of the world was coming to her aid. He must not see how much this was to her, how very much. She put out a little cold hand and laid it timidly in his big brown one, and he held it a moment and looked down at it in great tenderness, closed his fingers over it in a strong clasp, then laid it gently back in her lap as though it were too precious to keep. Her heart thrilled and thrilled again at his touch.

"Thank you," he said simply, a great withdrawing in his tone. "But I cannot see how you can think well of me. I am an utter stranger to you. I have no right to talk of such things to you."

"You did not tell me," answered Hazel. "You told—God." Her voice was slow and low with awe. "I only overheard. It was my fault—but—I am not—sorry. It was a great—thing to hear!"

He watched her shy dignity as she talked, her face drooping and half turned away. She was exquisitely beautiful in her confusion. His whole spirit yearned towards hers.

"I feel like a monster," he said suddenly. "You know I love you, but you do not understand how, in this short time even, you have filled my life, my whole being. And yet I may not ever try or hope to win your love in return. It must seem strange to you——''

"I think I understand," she said in a low voice; "you spoke of all that in the night—you know." It seemed as if she shrank from hearing it again.

"Will you let me explain it thoroughly to you?"

"If—you think best." She turned her face away and watched the eagle, now a mere speck in the distance.

"You see it is this way. I am not free to do as I might wish—as other men are free. I have consecrated my life to the service of God in this place. I know—I knew when I came here—that it was no place to bring a woman. There are few who could stand the life. It is filled with privations and hardships. They are inevitable. You are used to tender care and luxury. No man could ask a sacrifice like that of a woman he loved. He would not be a man if he did. It is not like marrying a girl who has felt the call herself, and loves to give her life to the work. That would be a different matter. But a man has no right to expect it of a woman——" he paused to find the right words and Hazel in a small still voice of dignity reminded him:

"You are forgetting one of the reasons."

"Forgetting?" he turned towards her wonderingly and their eyes met for just an instant, then hers were turned away again.

"Yes," she went on inscrutably. "You thought I—was not—fit!"

She was pulling up bits of green from the ground beside her. She felt a frightened flutter in her throat. It was the point of the thorn that had remained in her heart. It was not in nature for her not to speak of it, yet when it was spoken she felt how it might be misunderstood.

But the missionary made answer in a kind of cry like some hurt creature.

"Not fit! Oh, my dear! You do not understand——"

There was that in his tone that extracted the last bit of rankling thorn from Hazel's heart and brought the quick blood to her cheeks again.

With a light laugh that echoed with relief and a deep new joy which she dared not face as yet, she sprang to her feet.

"Oh, yes, I understand," she said gaily, "and it's all true. I'm not a bit fit for a missionary. But oughtn't we to be moving on? I'm quite rested now."

With a face that was grave to sadness he acquiesced, fastening the canvas in place on the saddle, and putting her on her horse with swift, silent movements. Then ,as she gathered up the reins he lingered for an instant and taking the hem of her gown in his fingers he stooped and touched his lips lightly, reverently to the cloth.

There was something so humble, so pathetic, so self-forgetful in the homage that the tears sprang to the girl's eyes and she longed to put her arms about his neck and draw his face close to hers and tell him how her heart was throbbing in sympathy.

But he had not even asked for her love, and there must be silence between them. He had shown that it was the only way. Her own reserve closed her lips and commanded that she show no sign.

And now they rode on silently for the most part, the horses' hoofs beating rapidly in unison. Now and then a rabbit scuttled on ahead of them or a horned toad hopped out of their path. Short brown lizards palpitated on bits of wood along the way; now and then a bright green one showed itself and disappeared. Once they came upon a village of prairie dogs and paused to watch their antics for a moment. It was then as they turned away that she noticed the bit of green he had stuck in his buttonhole and recognized it for the same that she had played with as they talked by the wayside. Her eyes charged him with having picked it up afterwards and his eyes replied with the truth, but they said no words about it. They did not need words.

It was not until they reached the top of a sloping hill, and suddenly came upon the view of the valley with its winding track gleaming in the late afternoon sun, the little wooden station and few cabins dotted here and there, that she suddenly realized that their journey together was at an end, for this was the place from which she had started two days before.

He had no need to tell her. She saw the smug red gleam of their own private car standing on the track not far away. She was brought face to face with the fact that her friends were down there in the valley and all the stiff conventionalities of

71

her life stood ready to build a wall between this man and herself. They would sweep him out of her life as if she had never met him, never been found and saved by him, and carry her away to their tiresome round of parties and pleasure excursions again.

She lifted her eyes with a frightened, almost pleading glance as if for a moment she would ask him to turn with her back to the desert again. She found his eyes upon her in a long deep gaze of farewell, as one looks upon the face of a beloved soon to be parted from earth. She could not bear the blinding of the love she saw there, and her own heart leaped up anew to meet it in answering love.

But it was only this one flash of a glance they had, when they were aware of voices and the sound of horses' hoofs, and almost instantly around the clump of sage-brush below the trail there swept into sight three horsemen, Shag Bunce, an Indian, and Hazel's brother. They were talking excitedly, and evidently starting out a new search.

The missionary with quick presence of mind started the horses on, shouting out a greeting, and was answered with instant cheers from the approaching party, followed by shots from Shag Bunce in signal that the lost was found; shots which immediately seemed to echo from the valley and swell into shouting and rejoicing.

Then all was confusion at once.

The handsome, reckless brother with gold hair like Hazel's embraced her, talking loud and eagerly; showing how he had done this and that to find her; blaming the country, the horses, the guides, the roads; and paying little heed to the missionary who instantly dropped behind to give him his place. It seemed but a second more before they were surrounded with eager people all talking at once, and Hazel, distressed that her brother gave so little attention to the man who had saved her, sought thrice to make some sort of an introduction, but the brother was too much taken up with excitement, and with scolding his sister for having gotten herself lost, to take it in.

Then out came the father, who, it appeared, had been up two nights on the search, and had been taking a brief nap. His face was pale and haggard. Brownleigh liked the look of his eyes as he caught sight of his daughter, and his face lighted s he saw her spring into his arms, crying: "Daddy! Daddy! 'm so sorry I frightened you!"

Behind him, tall and disapproving, with an I-told-you-so in er eye, stood Aunt Maria.

"Headstrong girl," she murmured severely. "You have given us all two terrible days!" and she pecked Hazel's cheek tiffly. But no one heard her in the excitement.

Behind Aunt Maria Hazel's maid wrung her hands and wept in a kind of hysterical joy over her mistress' return, and back of her in the gloom of the car vestibule loomed the dark countenance of Hamar with an angry, red mark across one cheek. He did not look particularly anxious to be there. The missionary turned from his evil face with repulsion.

In the confusion and delight over the return of the lost one he man of the desert prepared to slip away, but just as he was about to mount his pony Hazel turned and saw him.

"Daddy, come over here and speak to the man who found me and brought me safely back again," she said, dragging her father eagerly across the platform to where the missionary stood.

The father came readily enough and Hazel talked rapidly, her eyes shining, her cheeks like twin roses, telling in a breath of the horrors and darkness and rescue, and the thoughtfulness of her stranger-rescuer.

Mr. Radcliffe came forward with outstretched hand to greet him, and the missionary took off his hat and stood with easy grace to shake hands. He was not conscious then of the fire of eyes upon him, cold society stares from Aunt Maria, Hamar and young Radcliffe, as if to say, How dared he presume to expect recognition for doing what was a simple duty! He noted only the genuine heartiness in the face of the father as he thanked him for what he had done. Then, like the practical man of the world that he was, Mr. Radcliffe reached his hand into his pocket and drew out his check book remarking, as if it were a matter of course, that he wished to reward his daughter's rescuer handsomely, and inquiring his name as he pulled off the cap from his fountain pen.

Brownleigh stood back stiffly with a heightened colour, and an almost haughty look upon his face.

"Thank you," he said coldly, "I could not think of taking anything for a mere act of humanity. It was a pleasure to be able to serve your daughter," and he swung himself easily into the saddle.

But Mr. Radcliffe was unaccustomed to such independence in those who served him and he began to bluster. Hazel however, her cheeks fairly blazing, her eyes filled with mortification, put a hand upon her father's arm.

"Daddy, you don't understand," she said earnestly; "my new friend is a clergyman—he is a missionary, daddy!"

"Nonsense, daughter! You don't understand these matters. Just wait until I am through. I cannot let a deed like this go unrewarded. A missionary, did you say? Then if you won't take anything for yourself take it for your church; it's all the same in the end," and he gave a knowing wink towards the missionary whose anger was rising rapidly, and who was having much ado to keep a meek and quiet spirit.

"Thank you!" he said again coldly, "not for any such service."

"But I mean it!" grumbled the elder man much annoyed. "I want to donate something to a cause that employs a man like you. It is a good to the country at large to have such men patrolling the deserts. I never thought there was much excuse for Home Missions, but after this I shall give it my hearty approval. It makes the country safer for tourists. Come, tell me your name and I'll write out a check. I'm in earnest."

"Send any contribution you wish to make to the general fund," said Brownleigh with dignity, mentioning the address of the New York Board under whose auspices he was sent out, "but don't mention me, please." Then he lifted his hat once more and would have ridden away but for the distress in Hazel's eyes.

Just then the brother created a digression by rushing up to his father. "Dad, Aunt Maria wants to know if we can't go on, with this train. It's in sight now, and she is nearly crazy to get on the move. There's nothing to hinder our being hitched on, is there? The agent has the order. Do, dad, let's get out of this. I'm sick of it, and Aunt Maria is unbearable!"

"Yes, certainly, certainly, Arthur, speak to the agent. We'll go on at once. Excuse me, Mr.—— Ah, what did you say was the name? I'm sorry you feel that way about it; though it's very commendable, very commendable, I'm sure. I'll send to New York at once. Fifth Avenue, did you say?

I'll speak a good word for you. Excuse me. The agent is beckoning me. Well, goodbye, and thank you again! Daughter, you better get right into the car. The train is almost here, and they may have no time to spare,'' and Mr. Radcliffe hastened up the platform after his son and the agent.

IX

"For Remembrance"

Hazel turned her troubled eyes to the face of the man pleadingly. "My father does not understand," she said apologetically. "He is very grateful and he is used to thinking that money can always show gratitude."

Brownleigh was off his horse beside her, his hat off, before she had finished speaking.

"Don't, I beg of you, think of it again," he pleaded, his eyes devouring her face. "It is all right. I quite understand. And you understand too, I am sure."

"Yes, I understand," she said, lifting her eyes full of the love she had not dared to let him see. She was fidgetting with her rings as she spoke and looked back anxiously at the onrushing train. Her brother, hurrying down the platform to their car, called to her to hasten as he passed her, and she knew she would be allowed but a moment more. She caught her breath and looked at the tall missionary wistfully.

"You will let me leave something of my own with you, just for remembrance?" she asked eagerly.

His eyes grew tender and misty.

"Of course," he said, his voice suddenly husky, "though I shall need nothing to remember you by. I can never forget you." The memory of that look of his eyes was meat and drink to her soul during many days that followed, but she met it now steadily, not even flushing at her open recognition of his love.

"This is mine," she said. "My father bought it for me when I was sixteen. I have worn it ever since. He will never care." She slipped a ring from her finger and dropped it in his palm.

"Hurry up there, sister!" called young Radcliffe once more from the car window, and looking up, Brownleigh saw the evil face of Hamar peering from another window.

Hazel turned, struggling to keep back the rising tears. "I must go," she gasped.

Brownleigh flung the reins of the pony to a young Indian who stood near and turning walked beside her, conscious the while of the frowning faces watching them from the car windows.

"And I have nothing to give you," he said to her in a low tone, deeply moved at what she had done.

"Will you let me have the little book?" she asked shyly.

His eyes lit with a kind of glory as he felt in his pocket for his Bible.

"It is the best thing I own," he said. "May it bring you the same joy and comfort it has often brought to me." And he put the little book in her hand.

The train backed crashing up and jarred into the private car with a snarling, grating sound. Brownleigh put Hazel on the steps and helped her up. Her father was hurrying towards them and some train hands were making a great fuss shouting directions. There was just an instant for a hand-clasp, and then he stepped back to the platform, and her father swung himself on, as the train moved off. She stood on the top step of the car, her eyes upon his face, and his upon hers, his hat lifted in homage, and renunciation upon his brow as though it were a crown.

It was the voice of her Aunt Maria that recalled her to herself, while the little station with its primitive setting, its straggling onlookers and its one great man, slipped past and was blurred into the landscape by the tears which she could not keep back.

"Hazel! For pity's sake! Don't stand mooning and gazing at that rude creature any longer. We'll have you falling off the train and being dramatically rescued again for the delectation of the natives. I'm sure you've made disturbance enough for one trip, and you'd better come in and try to make amends to poor Mr. Hamar for what you have made him suffer with your foolish persistence in going off on a wild western pony that ran away. You haven't spoken to Mr. Hamar yet. Perhaps you don't know that he risked his life for you trying to catch your horse and was thrown and kicked in the face by his own wretched little beast, and left lying

77

unconscious for hours on the desert, until an Indian came along and picked him up and helped him back to the station." (As a matter of fact Milton Hamar had planned and enacted this touching drama with the help of a passing Indian, when he found that Hazel was gone, leaving an ugly whip mark on his cheek which must be explained to the family.) "He may bear that dreadful scar for life! He will think you an ungrateful girl if you don't go at once and make your apologies."

For answer Hazel, surreptitiously brushing away the tears, swept past her aunt and locked herself into her own little private stateroom.

She rushed eagerly to the window which was partly open, guarded with a screen, and pressed her face against the upper part of the glass. The train had described a curve across the prairie, and the station was still visible, though far away. She was sure she could see the tall figure of her lover standing with hat in hand watching her as she passed from his sight.

With quick impulse she caught up a long white crepe scarf that lay on her berth, and snatching the screen from the window fluttered the scarf out to the wind. Almost instantly a flutter of white came from the figure on the platform, and her heart quickened with joy. They had sent a message from heart to heart across the wide space of the plains, and the wireless telegraphy of hearts was established. Great tears rushed to blot the last flutter of white from the receding landscape, and then a hill loomed brilliant and shifting, and in a moment more shut out the sight of station and dim group and Hazel knew that she was back in the world of commonplace things once more, with only a memory for her company, amid a background of unsympathetic relatives.

She made her toilet in a leisurely way, for she dreaded to have to talk as she knew she would, and dreaded still more to meet Hamar. But she knew she must go and tell her father of her experiences, and presently she came out to them fresh and beautiful, with eyes but the brighter for her tears, and a soft wild-rose flush on her wind-browned cheeks that made her beauty all the sweeter.

They clamoured at once, of course, for all the details of her experience, and began by rehearsing once more how hard Mr. Hamar had tried to save her from her terrible plight, risking his life to stop her horse. Hazel said nothing to this, but one steady clear look at the disfigured face of the man who had made them believe all this was the only recognition she gave of his would-be heroism. In that look she managed to show her utter disbelief and contempt, though her Aunt Maria and perhaps even her father and brother thought her gratitude too deep for utterance before them all.

The girl passed over the matter of the runaway with a brief word, saying that the pony had made up his mind to run, and she had lost the bridle, which of course explained her inability to control him. She made light of her ride, however, before her aunt, and told the whole story most briefly until she came to the canyon and the howl of the coyotes. She was most warm in praise of her rescuer, though here too she used few words and avoided any description of the ride back, merely saying that the missionary had shown himself a gentleman in every particular, and had given her every care and attention that her own family could have done under the circumstances, making the way pleasant with stories of the country and the people. She said that he was a man of unusual culture and refinement, she thought, and yet most earnestly devoted to his work, and then she abruptly changed the subject by asking about certain plans for their further trip and seeming to have no further interest in what had befallen her; but all the while she was conscious of the piercing glance and frowning visage of Milton Hamar watching her, and she knew that as soon as opportunity offered itself he would continue the hateful interview begun on the plain. She decided mentally that she would avoid any such interview if possible, and to that end excused herself immmediately after lunch had been served, saying she needed a good sleep to make up for the long ride she had taken.

But it was not to sleep that she gave herself when she was at last able to take refuge in her little apartment again. She looked out at the passing landscape, beautiful with varied scenery, all blurred with tears as she thought of how she had but a little while before been out in its wide free distance with one who loved her. How that thought thrilled and thrilled her, and brought her a fresh joy each time it repeated itself! She wondered over the miracle of it. She never had dreamed that love was like this. She scarce believed it now. She was excited, stirred to the depths of her unusual experience, put

79

beyond the normal by the strangeness of the surroundings that had brought this man into her acquaintance; so said common sense, and warned her that to-morrow, or the next day, or at most next week, the thrill would all be gone and she would think of the stranger missionary as one curious detail of her Western trip. But her heart resented this, and down, deep down, something else told her this strange new joy would not vanish, that it would live throughout her life, and that whatever in the years came to her, she would always know underneath all that this had been the real thing, the highest fullness of a perfect love for her.

As the miles lengthened and her thoughts grew sad with the distance, she drew from its hiding place the little book he had given her at parting. She had slipped it into the breast pocket of her riding habit as she received it, for she shrank from having her aunt's keen eyes detect it and question her. She had been too much engrossed with the thought of separation to remember it till now.

She touched it tenderly, shyly, as though it were a part of himself; the limp, worn covers, the look of constant use, all made it inexpressibly dear. She had not known before that an inanimate object, not beautiful in itself, could bring such tender love.

Opening to the flyleaf, there in clear, bold writing was his name, "John Chadwick Brownleigh," and for the first time she realized that there had passed between them no word of her name. Strange that they two should have come so close as to need no names one with the other. But her heart leaped up with joy that she knew his name, and her eyes dwelt yearningly upon the written characters. John! How well the name fitted him. It seemed that she would have known it was his even if she had not seen it written first in one of his possessions. Then she fell to meditating whether he would have any way of discovering her name. Perhaps her father had given it to him, or the station agent might have known to whom their car belonged. Of course he would when he received the orders, —or did they give orders about cars only by numbers? She wished she dared ask some one. Perhaps she could find out in some way how those orders were written. And yet all the time she had an instinctive feeling that had he known her name a thousand times he would not have communicated with her. She knew by that exalted look of renunciation upon his face that no longing whatsoever could make him overstep the bounds which he had laid down between her soul and his.

With a sigh she opened the little book, and it fell apart of itself to the place where he had read the night before, the page still marked by the little silk cord he had placed so carefully. She could see him now with the firelight flickering on his face, and the moonlight silvering his head, that strong tender look upon his face. How wonderful he had been!

She read the psalm over now herself, the first time in her life she had ever consciously given herself to reading the Bible. But there was a charm about the words that gave them new meaning, the charm of his voice as she heard them in memory and watched again his face change and stir at the words as he read.

The day waned and the train flew on, but the landscape had lost its attraction now for the girl. She pleaded weariness and remained apart from the rest, dreaming over her wonderful experience, and thinking new deep thoughts of wonder, regret, sadness, joy, and when night fell and the great moon rose lighting the world again, she knelt beside her car window, looking long into the wide clear sky, the sky that covered him and herself; the moon that looked down upon them both. Then switching on the electric light over her berth she read the psalm once more, and fell asleep with her cheek upon the little book and in her heart a prayer for him.

John Brownleigh, standing upon the station platform, watching the train disappear behind the foot-hills, experienced, for the first time since his coming to Arizona, a feeling of the utmost desolation. Lonely he had been, and homesick, sometimes, but always with a sense that he was master of it all, and that with the delight of his work it would pass and leave him free and glad in the power wherewith his God had called him to the service. But now he felt that with this train the light of life was going from him, and all the glory of Arizona and the world in which he had loved to be was darkened on her account. For a moment or two his soul cried out that it could not be, that he must mount some winged steed and speed after her whom his heart had enthroned. Then the wall of the inevitable appeared before his eager eyes, and Reason crowded close to bring him to his senses. He turned away to hide the emotion in his face. The stolid Indian boy, who had been holding both horses, received his customary smile and pleasant word, but the missionary gave them more by habit than thought this time. His soul had entered its Gethsemane, and his spirit was bowed within him.

As soon as he could get away from the people about the station who had their little griefs and joys and perplexities to tell him, he mounted Billy, and leading the borrowed pony rode away into the desert, retracing the way they had come together but a short time before.

Billy was tired and walked slowly, drooping his head, and his master was sad at heart, so there was no cheerful converse between them as they travelled along.

It was not far they went, only back to the edge of the corn, where they had made their last stop of the journey together a few short hours before, and here the missionary halted and gave the beasts their freedom for a respite and refreshment. He himself felt too weary of soul to go further.

He took out the ring, the little ring that was too small to go more than half-way on his smallest finger, the ring she had taken warm and flashing from her white hand and laid within his palm!

The sun low down in the west stole into the heart of the jewel and sent its glory in a million multicoloured facets, piercing his soul with the pain and the joy of his love. He cast himself down upon the grass where she had sat, where, with his eyes closed and his lips upon the jewel she had worn, he met his enemy and fought his battle out.

Wearied at last with the contest, he slept. The sun went down, the moon made itself manifest once more, and when the night went coursing down its way of silver, two jewels softly gleamed in its radiance, the one upon his finger where he had pressed her ring, the other from the grass beside him. With a curious wonder he put forth his hand to the second and found it was the topaz set in the handle of her whip which she had dropped and forgotten when they sat together and talked by the way. He seized it eagerly now, and gathered it to him. It seemed almost a message of comfort from her he loved. It was something tangible, this, and the ring to show him he had not dreamed her coming; she had been real, and she had wanted him to tell her of his love, had said it would make a difference all the rest of her life.

He remembered that somewhere he had read or heard a great man say that to be worthy of a great love one must be able to do without it. Here now, then, he would prove his love by doing without. He stood with uplifted face, transfigured in the light of the brilliant night, with the look of exalted self-surrender, but only his heart communed that night, for there were no words on his dumb lips to express the fullness of his abnegation.

Then forth upon his way he went, his battle fought, the stronger for it, to be a staff for other men to lean upon.

X

His Mother

Deserts and mountains remain, duties crowd and press, hearts ache but the world rushes on. The weeks that followed showed these two that a great love is eternal.

Brownleigh did not try to put the thought of it out of his life, but rather let it glorify the common round. Day after day passed and he went from post to post, from hogan to mesa, and back to his shanty again, always with the thought of her companionship, and found it sweet. Never had he been less cheery when he met his friends, though there was a quiet dignity, a tender reserve behind it all that a few discerning ones perceived. They said at the Fort that he was losing flesh, but if so, he was gaining muscle. His lean brown arms were never stronger, and his fine strong face was never sad when any one was by. It was only in the night-time alone upon the moonlit desert, or in his little quiet dwelling place when he talked with his Father, and told all the loneliness and heartache. His people found him more sympathetic, more painstaking, more tireless than ever before, and the work prospered under his hand.

The girl in the city deliberately set herself to forget.

The first few days after she left him had been a season of ecstatic joy mingled with deep depression, as she alternately meditated upon the fact of a great love, or faced its impossibility.

She had scorched Milton Hamar with her glance of aversion, and avoided him constantly even in the face of protest from her family, until he had made excuse and left the party at Pasadena. There, too, Aunt Maria had relieved them of her annoying interference, and the return trip taken by the southern route had been an unmolested time for meditation for the girl. She became daily more and more dissatisfied with herself and her useless, ornamental life. Some days she read the little book, and other days she shut it away and tried to get back to her former life, telling herself it was useless to attempt to change herself. She had found that the little book gave her a deep unrest and a sense that life held graver, sweeter things than just living to please one's self. She began to long for home, and the summer round of gaieties, with which to fill the emptiness of her heart.

As the summer advanced there was almost a recklessness sometimes about the way she planned to have a good time every minute; yet in the quiet of her own room there would always come back the yearning that had been awakened in the desert and would not be silenced.

Sometimes when the memory of that great deep love she had heard expressed for herself came over her, the bitter tears would come to her eyes and one thought would throb through her consciousness: "Not worthy! Not worthy!" He had not thought her fit to be his wife. Her father and her world would think it quite otherwise. They would count him unworthy to mate with her, an heiress, the pet of society; he a man who had given up his life for a whim, a fad, a fanatical fancy! But she knew it was not so. She knew him to be a man of all men. She knew it was true that she was not such a woman as a man like that could fitly wed, and the thought galled her constantly.

She tried to accustom herself to think of him as a pleasant experience, a friend who might have been if circumstances with them both had been different; she tried to tell herself that it was a passing fancy with them which both would forget; and she tried with all her heart to forget, even locking away the precious little book and trying to forget it too.

And then, one day in late summer, she went with a motoring party through New England; as frolicsome and giddy a party as could be found among New York society transferred for the summer to the world of Nature. There was to be a dance or a house party or something of the sort at the end of the drive. Hazel scarcely knew, and cared less. She was becoming utterly weary of her butterfly life.

The day was hot and dusty, Indian summer intensified. They had got out of their way through a mistake of the chauffeur, and suddenly just on the edge of a tiny quaint little village the car broke down and refused to go on without a lengthy siege of coaxing and petting.

The members of the party, powdered with dust and in no very pleasant frame of mind from the delay, took refuge at the village inn, an old-time hostelry close to the roadside, with wide, brick-paved, white-pillared piazza across the front, and a mysterious hedged garden at the side. There were many plain wooden rockers neatly adorned with white crash on the piazza, and one or two late summer boarders loitering about with knitting work or book. The landlord brought cool tinkling glasses of water and rich milk from the spring-house, and they dropped into the chairs to wait while the men of the party gave assistance to the chauffeur in patching up the car.

Hazel sank warily into her chair and sipped the milk unhungrily. She wished she had not come; wished the day were over, and that she might have planned something more interesting; wished she had chosen different people to be of her party; and idly watched a white hen with yellow kid boots and a coral comb in her nicely groomed hair picking daintily about the green under the oak trees that shaded the street. She listened to the drone of the bees in the garden near by, the distant whetting of a scythe, the monotonous whang of a steam thresher not far away, the happy voices of children, and thought how empty a life in this village would be; almost as dreary and uninteresting as living in a desert—and then suddenly she caught a name and the pink flew into her cheeks and memory set her heart athrob.

It was the landlord talking to a lingering summer boarder, a quiet, gray-haired woman who sat reading at the end of the piazza.

"Well, Miss Norton, so you're goin' to leave us next week. Sorry to hear it. Don't seem nat'ral 'thout you clear through October. Ca'c'late you're comin' back to Granville in the spring?"

Granville! Granville! Where had she heard of Granville? Ah! She knew instantly. It was his old home! His mother lived there! But then of course it might have been another Granville. She wasn't even sure what state they were in now, New Hampshire or Vermont. They had been wavering about on the state line several times that day, and she never paid attention to geography.

Then the landlord raised his voice again.

He was gazing across the road where a white colonial house, white-fenced with pickets like clean sugar frosting, nestled in the luscious grass, green and clean and fresh, and seeming utterly apart from the soil and dust of the road, as if nothing wearisome could ever enter there. Brightly there bloomed a border of late flowers, double asters, zinnias, peonies, with a flame of scarlet poppies breaking into the smoke-like blue of larkspurs and bachelor buttons, as it neared the house. Hazel had not noticed it until now and she almost cried out with pleasure over the splendour of colour.

"Wal," said the landlord chinking some loose coins in his capacious pockets, "I reckon Mis' Brownleigh'll miss yeh 'bout as much as enny of us. She lots on your comin' over to read to her. I've heerd her say as how Amelia Ellen is a good nurse, but she never was much on the readin', an' Amelia Ellen knows it too. Mis' Brownleigh she'll be powerful lonesome fer yeh when yeh go. It's not so lively fur her tied to her bed er her chair, even ef John does write to her reg'lur twicet a week."

And now Hazel noticed that on the covered veranda in front of the wing of the house across the way there sat an old lady on a reclining wheeled chair, and that another woman in a plain blue gown hovered near waiting upon her. A luxuriant woodbine partly hid the chair, and the distance was too great to see the face of the woman, but Hazel grew weak with wonder and pleasure. She sat quite still trying to gather her forces while the summer boarder expressed earnest regret at having to leave her chosen summer abiding place so much earlier than usual. At last her friends began to rally Hazel on her silence. She turned away annoyed, and answered them crossly, following the landlord into the house and questioning him eagerly. She had suddenly arrived at the conclusion that she must see Mrs. Brownleigh and know if she looked like her son, and if she was the kind of mother one would expect such a son to have. She felt that in the sight might lie her emancipation from the bewitchment that had bound her in its toils since her Western trip. She also secretly hoped it might justify her dearest dreams of what his mother was like.

"Do you suppose that lady across the street would mind if I went over to look at her beautiful flowers?" she burst in upon the astonished landlord as he tipped his chair back with his feet on another and prepared to browse over yesterday's paper for the third time that day.

He brought his chair down on its four legs with a thump and drew his hat further over his forehead.

"Not a bit, not a bit, young lady. She's proud to show off her flowers. They're one of the sights of Granville. Mis' Brownleigh loves to have comp'ny. Jest go right over an' tell her I sent you. She'll tell you all about 'em, an' like ez not she'll give you a bokay to take 'long. She's real generous with 'em."

He tottered out to the door after her on his stiff rheumatic legs, and suggested that the other young ladies might like to go along, but they one and all declined, to Hazel's intense relief, and called their ridicule after her as she picked her way across the dusty road and opened the white gate into the peaceful scene beyond.

When she drew close to the side piazza she saw one of the most beautiful faces she had ever looked upon. The features were delicate and exquisitely modelled, aged by years and much suffering, yet lovely with a peace that had permitted no fretting. An abundance of waving silken hair white as driven snow was piled high upon her head against the snowy pillow, and soft brown eyes made the girl's heart throb quickly with their likeness to those other eyes that had once looked into hers.

She was dressed in a simple little muslin gown of white and gray with white cloud-like finish at throat and wrists, and across the helpless limbs was flung a light afghan of pink and gray wool. She made a sweet picture as she lay and watched her approaching guest with a smile of interest and welcome.

"The landlord said you would not mind if I came over to see your flowers," Hazel said with a shy, half-frightened catch in her voice. Now that she was here she was almost sorry she had come. It might not be his mother at all, and what could she say anyway? Yet her first glimpse told her that this was a mother to be proud of. "The most beautiful mother in the world" he had called her, and surely this woman could be none other than the one who had mothered such a son. Her highest ideals of motherhood seemed realized as she gazed upon the peaceful face of the invalid.

And then the voice! For the woman was speaking now, holding out a lily-white hand to her and bidding her be seated in the Chinese willow chair that stood close by the wheeled one; a great green silk cushion at the back, and a large palm leaf fan on the table beside it.

"I am so pleased that you came over," Mrs. Brownleigh was saying. "I have been wondering if some one wouldn't come to me. I keep my flowers partly to attract my friends, for I can stand a great deal of company since I'm all alone. You came in the big motor car that broke down, didn't you? I've been watching the pretty girls over there, in their gay ribbons and veils. They look like human flowers. Rest here and tell me where you have come from and where you are going, while Amelia Ellen picks you some flowers to take along. Afterwards you shall go among them and see if there are any you like that she has missed. Amelia Ellen! Get your basket and scissors and pick a great many flowers for this young lady. It is getting late and they have not much longer to blossom. There are three white buds on the rose-bush. Pick them all. I think they fit your face, my dear. Now take off your hat and let me see your pretty hair without its covering. I want to get your picture fixed in my heart so I can look at you after you are gone."

And so quite simply they fell into easy talk about each other, the day, the village, and the flowers.

"You see the little white church down the street? My husband was its pastor for twenty years. I came to this house a bride, and our boy was born here. Afterwards, when his father was taken away, I stayed right here with the people who loved him. The boy was in college then, getting ready to take up his father's work. I've stayed here ever since. I love the people and they love me, and I couldn't very well be moved, you know. My boy is out in Arizona, a home missionary!" She said it as Abraham Lincoln's mother might have said: "My boy is president of the United States!" Her face wore a kind of glory that bore a startling resemblance to the man of the desert. Hazel marvelled greatly, and understood what had made the son so great.

"I don't see how he could go and leave you alone!" she broke forth almost bitterly. "I should think his duty was here with his mother!"

"Yes, I know," the mother smiled; "they do say that, some of them, but it's because they don't understand. You see we gave John to God when he was born, and it was our hope from the first that he would choose to be a minister and a missionary. Of course John thought at first after his father went away that he could not leave me, but I made him see that I would be happier so. He wanted me to go with him, but I knew I should only be a hindrance to the work, and it came to me that my part in the work was to stay at home and let him go. It was all I had left to do after I became an invalid. And I'm very comfortable. Amelia Ellen takes care of me like a baby, and there are plenty of friends. My boy writes me beautiful letters twice a week, and we have such nice talks about the work. He's very like his father, and growing more so every day. Perhaps," she faltered and fumbled under the pink and silver lap robe, "perhaps you'd like to read a bit of one of his letters. I have it here. It came yesterday and I've only read it twice. I don't let myself read them too often because they have to last three days apiece at least. Perhaps you'd read it aloud to me. I like to hear John's words aloud sometimes and Amelia Ellen has never spent much time reading. She is peculiar in her pronunciation. Do you mind reading it to me?"

She held a letter forth, written in a strong free hand, the same that had signed the name John Chadwick Brownleigh in the little book. Hazel's heart throbbed eagerly and her hand trembled as she reached it shyly towards the letter. What a miracle was this! that his very letter was being put into her hand, her whom he loved—to read! Was it possible? Could there be a mistake? No, surely not. There could not be two John Brownleighs, both missionaries to Arizona.

"Dear little Mother o' Mine:" it began, and plunged at once into the breezy life of the Western country. He had been to a cattle round-up the week before and he described it minutely in terse and vivid language, with many a flash of wit, or graver touch of wisdom, and here and there a boyish expression that showed him young at heart, and devoted to his mother. He told of a visit he had paid to the Hopi Indians, their strange villages, each like a gigantic house with many rooms, called a pueblo, built on the edges of lofty crags or mesas and looking like huge castles five or six hundred feet above the desert floor. He told of Walpi, a village out on the end of a great promontory, its only access a narrow neck of land less than a rod wide, with one little path worn more than a foot deep in the solid rock by the feet of ten generations passing over it, where now live about two hundred and thirty people in one building. There were seven of these villages built on three mesas that reach out from the northern desert like three great fingers. Oraibi, the largest, having over a thousand people. He explained that Spanish explorers found these Hopis in 1540, long before the pilgrims landed at Plymouth Rock, and called the country Tusayan. Then he went on to describe a remarkable meeting that had been held in which the Indians had manifested deep interest in spiritual things, and had asked many curious questions about life, death and the hereafter.

"You see, dear," said the mother, her eyes shining eagerly, "you see how much they need him, and I'm glad I can give him. It makes me have a part in the work."

Hazel turned back to the letter and went on reading to hide the tears that were gathering in her own eyes as she looked upon the exalted face of the mother.

There was a detailed account of a conference of missionaries, to attend which the rider had ridden ninety miles on horseback; and at the close there was an exquisite description of the spot where they had camped the last night of their ride. She knew it from the first word almost, and her heart beat so wildly she could hardly keep her voice steady to read:

"I stopped over night on the way home at a place I dearly love. There is a great rock, shelving and overhanging, for shelter from any passing storm, and quite near a charming green boudoir of cedars on three sides, and rock on the fourth. An abundant waterhole makes camping easy for me and Billy, and the stars overhead are good tapers. Here I build my fire and boil the kettle, read my portion and lie down to watch the heavens. Mother, I wish you knew how near to God one feels out in the desert with the stars. Last night about three o'clock I woke to replenish my fire and watch a while a great comet, the finest one for many years. I would tell you about it but I've already made this letter too long, and it's time Billy and I were on our way again. I love this spot beside the big rock and often come back to it on my journeys; perhaps because here I once camped with a dear friend and we had pleasant converse together around our brushwood fire. It makes the desert seem less lonely because I can sometimes fancy my friend still reclining over on the other side of the fire in the light that plays against the great rock. Well, little mother o' mine, I must close. Cheer up, for it has been intimated to me that I may be sent East to General Assembly in the spring, and then for three whole weeks with you! That will be when the wild strawberries are out, and I shall carry you in my arms and spread a couch for you on the strawberry hill behind the house, and you shall pick some again with your own hands.''

With a sudden catch in her throat like a sob the reading came to an end and Hazel, her eyes bright with tears, handed the letter reverently back to the mother whose face was bright with smiles.

"Isn't he a boy worth giving?" she asked as she folded the letter and slipped it back under the pink and gray cover.

"He is a great gift," said Hazel in a low voice.

She was almost glad that Amelia Ellen came up with an armful of flowers just then and she might bury her face in their freshness and hide the tears that would not be stayed, and then before she had half admired their beauty there was a loud ''Honk-honk!'' from the road, followed by a more impatient one, and Hazel was made aware that she was being waited for.

"I'm sorry you must go, dear," said the gentle woman. "I haven't seen so beautiful a girl in years, and I'm sure you have a lovely heart, too. I wish you could visit me again."

"I will come again some time if you will let me!" said the girl impulsively, and then stooped and kissed the soft rose-leaf cheek, and fled down the path trying to get control of her emotion before meeting her companions.

Hazel was quiet all the rest of the way, and was rallied much upon her solemnity. She pleaded a headache and closed her eyes, while each heart-throb carried her back over the months and brought her again to the little camp under the rock beneath the stars.

"He remembered still! He cared!" This was what her glad thoughts sang as the car whirled on, and her gay companions forgot her and chattered of their frivolities.

"How wonderful that I should find his mother!" she said again and again to herself. Yet it was not so wonderful. He had told her the name of the town, and she might have come here any time of her own accord. But it was strange and beautiful that the accident had brought her straight to the door of the house where he had been born and brought up! What a beautiful, happy boyhood he must have had with a mother like that! Hazel found herself thinking wistfully, out of the emptiness of her own motherless girlhood. Yes, she would go back and see the sweet mother some day; and she fell to planning how it could be.

XI

Refuge

Milton Hamar had not troubled Hazel all summer. From time to time her father mentioned him as being connected with business enterprises, and it was openly spoken of now that a divorce had been granted him, and his former wife was soon to marry again. All this, however, was most distasteful to the girl to whom the slightest word about the man served to bring up the hateful scene of the desert.

But early in the fall he appeared among them again, assuming his old friendly attitude towards the whole family, dropping in to lunch or dinner whenever it suited his fancy. He seemed to choose to forget what had passed between Hazel and himself, to act as though it had not been, and resumed his former playful attitude of extreme interest in the girl of whom he had always been fond. Hazel, however, found a certain air of proprietorship in his gaze, a too-open expression of his admiration which was offensive. She could not forget, try as hard as she might for her father's sake to forgive. She shrank away from the man's company, avoided him whenever possible, and at last when he seemed to be almost omnipresent, and growing every day more insistent in his attentions, she cast about her for some absorbing interest which would take her out of his sphere.

Then a strange fancy took her in its possession.

It was in the middle of the night when it came to her, where she had been turning her luxurious pillow for two hours trying in vain to tempt a drowsiness that would not come, and she arose at once and wrote a brief and business-like letter to the landlord of the little New Hampshire inn where she had been delayed for a couple of hours in the fall. In the morning, true to her impulsive nature, she besieged her father until he gave his permission for her to take her maid and a quiet elderly cousin of his and go away for a complete rest before the society season began.

It was a strange whim for his butterfly daughter to take but the busy man saw no harm in it, and was fully convinced that it was merely her way of punishing some over ardent follower for a few days; and feeling sure she would soon return, he let her go. She had had her way all her life, and why should he cross her in so simple a matter as a few days' rest in a country inn with a respectable chaperone?

The letter to the landlord was outtravelled by a telegram whose answer sent Hazel on her way the next morning, thankful that she had been able to get away during a temporary absence of Milton Hamar, and that her father had promised not to let any of her friends know of her whereabouts. His eye had twinkled as he made the promise. He was quite sure which of her many admirers was being punished, but he did not tell her so. He intended to be most judicious with all her young men friends. He so confided his intentions to Milton Hamar that evening, having no thought that Hazel would mind their old friend's knowing.

Two days later Hazel, after establishing her little party comfortably in the best rooms the New Hampshire inn afforded, putting a large box of new novels at their disposal, and another of sweets, and sending orders for new magazines to be forwarded, went over to call on the sweet old lady towards whom her heart had been turning eagerly, with a longing that would not be put away, ever since that first accidental, or providential, meeting.

When she came back, through the first early snow-storm, with her cheeks like winter roses and her furry hat all feathered with great white flakes, she found Milton Hamar seated in front of the open fire in the office making the air heavy with his best tobacco, and frowning impatiently through the small-paned windows.

The bright look faded instantly from her face and the peace which she had almost caught from the woman across the way. Her eyes flashed indignantly, and her whole small frame stiffened for the combat that she knew must come now. There was no mistaking her look. Milton Hamar knew at once that he was not welcome. She stood for an instant with the door wide open, blowing a great gust of biting air across the wide room and into his face. A cloud of smoke sprang out from the fireplace to meet it and the two came together in front of the man, and made a visible wall for a second between him and the girl.

He sprang to his feet, cigar in hand, and an angry exclamation upon his lips. The office, fortunately, was without other occupant.

"Why in the name of all that's unholy did you lead me a race away off to this forsaken little hole in midwinter, Hazel?" he cried.

Hazel drew herself to her full height and with the dignity that well became her, answered him:

"Really, Mr. Hamar, what right have you to speak to me in that way? And what right had you to follow me?"

"The right of a man who is going to marry you!" he answered fiercely; "and I think it's about time this nonsense stopped. It's nothing but coquettish foolishness, your coming here. I hate coquettish fools. I didn't think you had it in you to coquet, but it seems all women are alike."

"Mr. Hamar, you are forgetting yourself," said the girl quietly, turning to shut the door that she might gain time to get control of her shaken nerves. She had a swift vision of what it would be if she were married to a man like that. No wonder his wife was entirely willing to give him a divorce. But she shuddered as she turned back and faced him bravely.

"Well, what did you come here for?" he asked in a less fierce tone.

"I came because I wanted to be quiet," Hazel said trying to steady her voice, "and—I will tell you the whole truth. I came because I wanted to get away from—you! I have not liked the way you acted towards me since—that day—in Arizona."

The man's fierce brows drew together, but a kind of mask of apology overspread his features. He perceived that he had gone too far with the girl whom he had thought scarcely more than a child. He had thought he could mould her like wax, and that his scorn would instantly wither her wiles. He watched her steadily for a full minute; the girl, though trembling in every nerve, sending back a steady, haughty gaze.

"Do you mean that?" he said at last.

"I do!" Her voice was quiet, but she was on the verge of tears.

"Well, perhaps we'd better talk it over. I see I've taken too much for granted. I thought you'd understood for a year or more what was going on—what I was doing it for."

"You thought I understood! You thought I would be willing to be a party to such an awful thing as you have done!" Hazel's eyes were flashing fire now. The tears were scorched away.

"Sit down! We'll talk it over," said the man moving a great summer chair nearer to his own. His eyes were on her face approvingly and he was thinking what a beautiful picture she made in her anger.

"Never!" said the girl quickly. "It is not a thing I could talk over. I do not wish to speak of it again. I wish you to leave this place at once," and she turned with a quick movement and fled up the quaint old staircase.

She stayed in her room until he left, utterly refusing to see him, refusing to answer the long letters he wrote and sent up to her; and finally, after another day, he went away. But he wrote to her several times, and came again twice, each time endeavouring to surprise her into talking with him. The girl grew to watch nervously every approach of the daily stage which brought stray travellers from the station four miles distant, and was actually glad when a heavy snow-storm shut them in and made it unlikely that her unwelcome visitor would venture again into the country.

The last time he came Hazel saw him descending from the coach, and without a word to any one, although it was almost supper time, and the early winter twilight was upon them, she seized her fur cloak and slipped down the back stairs, out through the shadows, across the road, where she surprised good Amelia Ellen by flinging her arms about her neck and bursting into tears right in the dark front hall, for the gust of wintry wind from the open door blew the candle out, and Amelia Ellen stood astonished and bewildered for a moment in the blast of the north wind with the soft arms of the excited girl in her furry wrappings clinging about her unaccustomed shoulders.

Amelia Ellen had never had many beautiful things in her life, the care of her Dresden-china mistress, and her brilliant garden of flowers, having been the crowning of her life hitherto. This beautiful city girl with her exquisite garments and her face like a flower, flung upon her in sudden appeal, drew out all the latent love and pity and sympathy of which Amelia Ellen had a larger store than most, hidden under a simple and severe exterior.

"Fer the land's sake! Whatever ails you!" she exclaimed when she could speak for astonishment, and to her own surprise her arm enclosed the sobbing girl in a warm embrace while with the other hand she reached to close the door. "Come right in to my kitchen and set in the big chair by the cat and let me give you a cup o' tea. Then you can tell Mis' Brownleigh what's troublin' you. She'll know how to talk to you. I'll git you some tea right away."

She drew the shrinking girl into the kitchen and ousting the cat from a patchwork rocker pushed her gently into it. It was characteristic of Amelia Ellen that she had no thoughts of ministering to her spiritual needs herself, but knew her place was to bring physical comfort.

She spoke no word save to the cat, admonishing him to mend his manners and keep out from under foot, while she hurried to the tea canister, the bread box, the sugar bowl, and the china closet. Soon a cup of fragrant tea was set before the unexpected guest, and a bit of delicate toast browning over the coals, to be buttered and eaten crisp with the tea; and the cat nestled comfortably at Hazel's feet while she drank the tea and wiped away the tears.

"You'll think I'm a big baby, Amelia Ellen!" cried Hazel trying to smile shamedly "but I'm just so tired of the way things go. You see somebody I don't a bit like has come up from New York on the evening coach, and I've run away for a little while. I don't know what made me cry. I never cry at home, but when I got safely over here a big lump came in my throat and you looked so nice and kind that I couldn't keep the tears back."

From that instant Amelia Ellen, toasting fork in hand, watching the sweet blue eyes and the tear-stained face that resembled a drenched pink bud after a storm, loved Hazel Radcliffe. Come weal, come woe, Amelia Ellen was from henceforth her staunch admirer and defendant.

"Never you mind, honey, you just eat your tea an' run in

to Mis' Brownleigh, an' I'll get my hood an' run over to tell your folks you've come to stay all night over here. Then you'll have a cozy evenin' readin' while I sew, an' you can sleep late come mornin', and go back when you're ready. Nobody can't touch you over here. I'm not lettin' in people by night 'thout I know 'em,'' and she winked knowingly at the girl by way of encouragement. Well she knew who the unwelcome stranger from New York was. She had keen eyes, and had watched the coach from her well-curtained kitchen window as it came in.

That night Hazel told her invalid friend all about Milton Hamar, and slept in the pleasant bed that Amelia Ellen had prepared for her, with sheets of fragrant linen redolent of sweet clover. Her heart was lighter for the simple, kindly advice and the gentle love that had been showered upon her. She wondered, as she lay half dozing in the morning with the faint odour of coffee and muffins penetrating the atmosphere, why it was that she could love this beautiful mother of her hero so much more tenderly than she had ever loved any other woman. Was it because she had never known her own mother and had longed for one all her life, or was it just because she was *his* dear mother? She gave up trying to answer the question and went smiling down to breakfast, and then across the road to face her unwelcome lover, strong in the courage that friendly counsel had given her.

Milton Hamar left before dinner, having been convinced at last of the uselessness of his visit. He hired a man with a horse and cutter to drive him across country to catch the New York evening express, and Hazel drew a breath of relief and began to find new pleasure in life. Her father was off on a business trip for some weeks; her brother had gone abroad for the winter with a party of college friends. There was no real reason why she should return to New York for some time, and she decided to stay and learn of this saintly woman how to look wisely on the things of life. To her own heart she openly acknowledged that there was a deep pleasure in being near one who talked of the man she loved.

So the winter settled down to business, and Hazel spent happy days with her new friends, for Amelia Ellen had become a true friend in the best sense of the word.

The maid had found the country winter too lonely and

Hazel had found her useless and sent her back to town. She was learning by association with Amelia Ellen to do a few things for herself. The elderly cousin, whose years had been a long strain of scrimping to present a respectable exterior, was only too happy to have leisure and quiet to read and embroider to her heart's content. So Hazel was free to spend much time with Mrs. Brownleigh.

They read together, at least Hazel did the reading, for the older eyes were growing dim, and had to be guarded to prevent the terrible headaches which came at the slightest provocation and made the days a blank of suffering for the lovely soul where patience was having its perfect work.

The world of literature opened through a new door to the eager young mind now. Books of which she had never heard were at her hand. New thoughts and feelings were stirred by them. A few friends who knew Mrs. Brownleigh through their summer visits, and others who had known her husband, kept her well supplied with the latest and always the best of everything—history, biography, essays and fiction. But there were also books of a deep spiritual character, and magazines that showed a new world, the religious world, to the girl. She read with zest all of them, and enjoyed deeply the pleasant converse concerning each. Her eyes were being opened to new ways of living. She was beginning to know that there was an existence more satisfying than just to go from one round of amusement to another. And always, more than in any other thing she read, she took a most unusual interest in home missionary literature. It was not because it was so new and strange and like a fairy tale, nor because she knew her friend enjoyed hearing all this news so much, but because it held for her the story of the man she now knew she loved, and who had said he loved her. She wanted to put herself into touch with surroundings like his, to understand better what he had to endure, and why he had not dared to ask her to share his life, his hardship—most of all why he had not thought her worthy to suffer with him.

When she grew tired of reading she would go out into the kitchen and help Amelia Ellen. It was her own whim that she should learn how to make some of the good things to eat for which Amelia Ellen was famous. So while her society friends at home went from one gay scene to another, dancing and frivolling through the night and sleeping away the morning, Hazel bared her round white arms, enveloped herself in a clean blue-checked apron, and learned to make bread and pies and gingerbread and puddings and doughnuts and fruit-cake, how to cook meats and vegetables and make delicious broths from odds and ends, and to concoct the most delectable desserts that would tempt the frailest appetite. Real old country things they were—no fancy salads and whips and froths that society has hunted out to tempt its waning taste till everything has palled. She wrote to one of her old friends, who demanded to know what she was doing so long up there in the country in the height of the season, that she was taking a course in Domestic Science and happily recounted her menu of accomplishments. Secretly her heart rejoiced that she was become less and less unworthy of the love of the man in whose home and at whose mother's side she was learning sweet lessons.

There came letters, of course, from the faraway missionary. Hazel stayed later in the kitchen the morning of their arrival, conscious of a kind of extra presence in his mother's room when his letters arrived. She knew the mother liked to be alone with her son's letters, and that she saved her eyes from other reading for them alone. Always the older face wore a kind of glorified look when the girl entered after she had been reading her letter. The letter itself would be hidden away out of sight in the bosom of her soft gray gown, to be read again and again when she was alone, but seldom was it brought out in the presence of the visitor, much as the mother was growing to love this girl. Frequently there were bits of news.

"My son says he is very glad I am having such delightful company this winter, and he wants me to thank you from him for reading to me," she said once, patting Hazel's hand as she tucked the wool robe about her friend's helpless form. And again:

"My son is starting to build a church. He is very happy about it. They have heretofore held worship in a schoolhouse. He has collected a good deal of the money himself, and he will help to put up the building with his own hands. He is going to send me a photograph when it is up. I would like to be present when it is dedicated. It makes me very proud to have my son doing that."

The next letter brought a photograph, a small snapshot of the canyon, tiny, but clear and distinct. Hazel's hand trembled when the mother gave it to her to look at, for she knew the very spot. She fancied it was quite near the place where they had paused for water. She could feel again the cool breath of the canyon, the damp smell of the earth and ferns, and hear the call of the wild bird.

Then one day there came a missionary magazine with a short article on the work of Arizona and a picture of the missionary mounted on Billy, just ready to start from his little shack on a missionary tour.

Hazel, turning the leaves, came upon the picture and held her breath with astonishment and delight; then rapidly glanced over the article, her heart beating wildly as though she had heard his voice suddenly calling to her out of the distances that separated them. She had a beautiful time surprising the proud mother with the picture and reading the article. From that morning they seemed to have a tenderer tie between them, and once, just before Hazel was leaving for the night, the mother reached out a detaining hand and laid it on the girl's arm. "I wish my boy and you were acquainted, dear," she said wistfully. And Hazel, the rich colour flooding her face at once, replied hesitatingly:

"Oh, why—I—feel—almost—as—though—we *were!*" Then she kissed her friend on the soft cheek and hurried back to the inn.

It was that night that the telegram came to say that her father had been seriously injured in a railway accident and would be brought home at once. She had no time to think of anything then but to hurry her belongings together and hasten to New York.

XII

Qualifying for Service

During the six weeks' lingering suffering that followed the accident Hazel was never far from her father's bedside. It seemed as though a new bond of understanding had come between them.

He was very low and there was little hope from the beginning. As he grew weaker he seemed never to want his daughter out of sight, and once when he woke suddenly to find her close beside him, a smile of relief spread over his face, and he told her in brief words that he had dreamed she was lost again in Arizona, and that he had been searching for her with the wild beasts howling all about and wicked men prowling in dark caves. He told her how during that awful time of her disappearance he had been haunted by her face as she was a tiny baby after her mother died, and it seemed to him he should go mad if he could not find her at once.

Then to soothe him she told him of the missionary, and how gently he had cared for her; told him of all the pleasant little details of the way, though not, of course, of his love for her nor hers for him. Perhaps the father, with eyes keen from their nearness to the other world, discerned something of her interest as she talked, for once he sighed and said, in reference to the life of sacrifice the missionary was leading: "Well, I don't know but such things are more worth while after all."

And then with sudden impulse she told him of her finding his mother, and why she had wanted to go to the country in the middle of the society season, because she wanted to know more of the peaceful life this woman lived.

"Perhaps you will meet him again. Who knows?" said the father, looking wistfully at his lovely daughter, and then he turned his head away and sighed again.

As the confidence grew between them she told him one day of Milton Hamar's unwelcome proposal, and the indignation of the father knew no bounds.

It was after that she ventured to read to him from the little book, and to tell of the worship held out under the stars in the desert. It came to be a habit between them, as the days grew less, that she should read the little book, and afterwards he would always lie still as if he were asleep.

It was on the words of the precious psalm that he closed his eyes for the last time in this world, and it was the psalm that brought comfort to the daughter's heart when she came back to the empty house after the funeral.

Her brother was there, it is true, but he was afraid of death, and wanted to get back to his world again, back to the European trip where he had left his friends, and especially a gay young countess who had smiled upon him. He was impatient of death and sorrow. Hazel saw that he could not comprehend her loneliness, so she bade him go as soon as decency would allow, and he was not long in obeying her. He had had his own way all his life, and even death was not to deny him.

The work of the trained nurses who had cared for her father interested Hazel deeply. She had talked with them about their life and preparation for it, and when she could no longer stand the great empty house with only Aunt Maria for company, who had come back just before Mr. Radcliffe's death, she determined to become a nurse herself.

There was much ado over her decision among her acquaintances, and Aunt Maria thought it was not quite respectable for her to do so eccentric a thing and so soon after her father's death. She would have preferred to have had her run down to Lakewood for a few weeks and then follow her brother across the water for a year or two of travel; but Hazel was quite determined, and before January was over she was established in the hospital, through the influence of their family physician, and undergoing her first initiation.

It was not easy thus to give up her life of doing exactly as she pleased when she pleased, and become a servant under orders. Her back often ached, and her eyes grew heavy with the watching and the ministering, and she would be almost ready to give over. Then the thought of the man of the desert gave her new courage and strength. It came to her that she was partaking with him in the great work of the kingdom, and with this thought she would rise and go about the strange new work again, until her interest in the individuals to whom she ministered grew deep, and she understood in a measure the reason for the glory in the face of the missionary as he spoke in the starlight about his work.

Often her heart went out wistfully towards her invalid friend in New Hampshire, and she would rest herself by writing a long letter, and would cherish the delicately written answers. Now and again there would be some slight reference to "my son" in these letters. As the spring came on they were more frequent, for May would bring the General Assembly, and the son was to be one of the speakers. How her heart throbbed when she read that this was certain now. A few days later when she happened to read in the daily paper some item about Assembly plans and discovered for the first time that it was to meet in New York, she found herself in a flutter of joy. Would it be possible for her to hear him speak? That was the great question that kept coming and going in her mind. Could she arrange it so that she would be sure to be off duty when his time came to speak? How could she find out about it all? Thereafter her interest in the church news of the daily papers became deep.

Then spring came on with its languid air and the hard round of work, with often a call to watch when overcome with weariness, or to do some unaccustomed task that tried her undisciplined soul. But the papers were full of the coming Assembly, and at last the program and his name!

She laid her plans most carefully, but the case she had been put upon that week was very low, dying, and the woman had taken a fancy to her and begged her to stay by her till the end. It was a part of the new Hazel that she stayed, though her heart rose up in protest and tears of disappointment would keep coming to her eyes. The head nurse marked them with disapproval and told the house doctor that Radcliffe would never make much of a nurse; she had no control over her emotions.

Death came, almost too late, and set her free for the afternoon, but it was but half an hour to the time set for his speech, she was three miles from the place of meeting and still in her uniform. It was almost foolish to try. Nevertheless she hurried to her room and slipped into a plain little street suit, the thing that would go on quickest, and was away.

It seemed as though every cab and car and mode of transit had conspired to hinder her, and five minutes before the time set for the next speech she hurried breathless into the dim hallway of a great crowded church, and pressed up the stairs to the gallery, through the silent leather doors that could scarcely swing open for the crowd inside then she heard at last—*his* voice!

She was away up at the top of the gallery. Men and women were standing close all about her. She could not catch even a glimpse of the platform with its array of noble men whose consecration and power and intellects had made them great religious leaders. She could not see the young commanding figure standing at the edge of the platform, nor catch the flash of his brown eyes as he held the audience in his power while he told the simple story of his Western work; but she could hear the voice, and it went straight to her lonely, sorrowful heart. Straightway the church with its mass of packed humanity, its arched and carven ceiling, its magnificent stained-glass windows, its wonderful organ and costly fittings, faded from her sight, and overhead there arched a dome of dark blue pierced with stars, and mountains in the distance with a canyon opening, and a flickering fire. She heard the voice speak from its natural setting, though her eyes were closed and full of tears.

He finished his story amid a breathless silence on the part of his audience, and then with scarcely a break in his voice spoke to God in one of his uplifting prayers. The girl, trembling, almost sobbing, felt herself included in the prayer, felt again the protection of an unseen Presence, felt the benediction in his voice as he said, "Amen," and echoed its utmost meaning in her soul.

The audience was still hushed as the speaker turned to go to his seat at the back of the platform. A storm of applause had been made impossible by that prayer, for heaven opened with the words and God looked down and had to do with each soul present. But the applause burst forth after all in a moment, for the speaker had whispered a few words to the moderator and was hurrying from the platform. There were ries of, "Don't go! Tell us more! Keep on till six o'clock!" Hazel could not see a thing though she stretched her neck and stood upon the tips of her toes, but she clasped her hands tightly together when the applause came, and her heart echoed every sound.

The clamour ceased a moment as the moderator raised his hand, and explained that the brother to whom they had all been listening with such pleasure would be glad to speak to them longer, but that he was hastening away to take the train to see his invalid mother who had been waiting for two long years for her boy. A pause, a great sigh of sympathy and disappointment, and then the applause burst forth again, and continued till the young missionary had left the church.

Hazel, in bitter disappointment, turned and slipped out. She had not caught a glimpse of his beloved face. She exulted that she had heard the honour given him, been a part of those who rejoiced in his power and consecration, but she could not have him go without having at least oné look at him.

She hurried blindly down the stairs, out to the street, and saw a carriage standing before the door. The carriage door had just been closed, but as she gazed he turned and looked out for an instant, lifting his hat in farewell to a group of ministers who stood on the church steps. Then the carriage whirled him away and the world grew suddenly blank.

She had been behind the men on the steps, just within the shadow of the dim doorway. He had not seen her, and of course would not have recognized her if he had; yet now she realized that she had hoped—oh—what had she not hoped from meeting him here!

But he was gone, and it might be years before he came East again. He had utterly put her from his life. He would not think of her again if he did come! Oh, the loneliness of a world like this! Why, oh why, had she ever gone to the desert to learn the emptiness of her life, when there was no other for her anywhere!

The days that followed were very sad and hard. The only thought that helped now was that she too had tried to give her life for something worth while as he had done, and perhaps it might be accepted. But there was a deep unrest in her soul now, a something that she knew she had not got that she longed inexpressibly to have. She had learned to cook and to nurse. She was not nearly so useless as when she rode a care-free upon the desert. She had overcome much of he unworthiness. But there was still one great obstacle which unfitted her for companionship and partnership with the ma of the desert. She had not the something in her heart and lif that was the source and centre of self-sacrifice. She was sti unworthy.

There was a long letter about the first of June from he friend in New Hampshire, more shakily written, she fancied than those that had come before, and then there came a interval without any reply to hers. She had little time, howev er, to worry about it, for the weather was unusually warm an the hospital was full. Her strength was taxed to its utmost t fill her round of daily duties. Aunt Maria scolded and insiste on a vacation, and finally in high dudgeon betook herself t Europe for the summer. The few friends with whom Haze kept up any intercourse hurried away to mountains or sea and the summer settled down to business.

And now in the hot, hot nights when she lay upon he small bed, too weary almost to sleep, she would fancy sh heard again that voice as he spoke in the church, or longe ago in the desert; and sometimes she could think she felt th breeze of the desert night upon her hot forehead.

The head nurse and the house doctor decided Radcliff needed a change and suggested a few days at the shore with convalescing patient, but Hazel's heart turned from the thought and she insisted upon sticking to her post. She clung to th thought that she could at least be faithful. It was what h would do, and in so much she would be like him, and worth of his love.

It was the last thought in her mind before she fainted on the broad marble staircase with a tiny baby in her arms, and fel to the bottom. The baby was uninjured, but it took a lon time to bring the nurse back to consciousness, and still longe to put heart into her again.

"She isn't fit for the work!" she heard the biting tongue o the head nurse declare. "She's too frail and pretty and— emotional. She feels everybody's troubles. Now I never let case worry me in the least!" And the house doctor eyed he knowingly and said in his heart:

"Any one would know that."

But Hazel, listening, was more disheartened than ever. Then here, too, she was failing and was adjudged unworthy!

The next morning there came a brief, blunt note from Amelia Ellen: "Dear Mis Raclift Ef yore a trainurse why don't yo cum an' take car o' my Mis Brownleigh She aint ong fer heer an she's wearyin to see yo She as gotta hev one, a trainurse I mean Yors respectfooly Amelia Ellen Stout."

After an interview with the house doctor and another with her old family physician, Hazel packed up her uniforms and departed for New Hampshire.

It was the evening of her arrival, after the gentle invalid had been prepared for sleep and left in the quiet and dark, that Amelia Ellen told the story:

"She ain't ben the same since John went back. Seems like she sort o' sensed thet he wouldn't come again while she was livin'. She tole me the next day a lot of things she wanted done after she was gone, and she's ben gettin' ready to leave this earth ever since. Not that she's gloomy, oh, my senses no! She's jes' as interested as can be in her flowers, and in folks, an' the church, but she don't want to try to do so many things, and she has them weak, fainty spells oftener, an' more pain in her heart. She sits fer long hours with jest her Bible open now, but land, she don't need to read it! She knows it most by heart—that is the livin' parts, you know. She don't seem to care 'tall fer them magazine articles now any more. I wish t' the land they'd be anuther Gen'l 'Sembly! Thet was the greatest thing fer her. She jest acted like she was tendin' every blessed one o' them meetin's. Why, she couldn't wait fer me t' git done my breakfast dishes. She'd want me t' fix her up fer the day, an' then set down an' read their doin's. 'We kin let things go, you know, 'Meelia Ellen,' she'd say with her sweet smile, 'just while the meetin's last. Then when it's over they'll be time 'nough fer work—an' rest too 'Meelia Ellen,' says she. Well, seems like she was just tendin' those meetin's herself, same es if she was there. She'd take her nap like it was a pill, er somethin', and then be wide awake an' ready fer her afternoon freshenin', an' then she'd watch fer the stage to bring the evenin' paper. John, he hed a whole cartload o' papers sent, an' the day he spoke they was so many I jes' couldn't get my bread set. I hed to borry a loaf off the inn. First time that's ever happened to me either. I jest hed to set an' read till my back ached, an' my eyes swum. I never read so much in my whole borned days t' oncet; an' I've done a good bit o' readin' in my time too, what with nursin' her an' bein' companion to a perfessor' invaleed daughter one summer.

"Wal, seems like she jest went on an' on, gettin' workeder up an' workeder-up, till the 'Sembly closed, an' he come and she was clear to the top o' the heap all them three week whilst he was here. Why, I never seen her so bright since when I was a little girl an' went to her Sunday-school class an' she wore a poke bonnet trimmed with lutestring ribbon an' a rose inside. Talk 'bout roses—they wasn't one in the garden as bright an' pink as her two cheeks, an' her eye shone jest fer all the world like his. I was terrible troubled lest she'd break down, but she didn't. She got brighter an' brighter. Let him take her out ridin', an' let him carry her into the orchard an' lay her down under the apple boughs where she could reach a wild strawberry herself. Why, she hedn' ben off'n the porch sence he went away two years ago. But every day he stayed she got brighter. The last day 'fore he left she seemed like she wasn't sick at all. She wanted to get up early, an' she wouldn't take no nap, 'cause she said she couldn't waste a minute of the last day. Well, she actu'lly go on her feet oncet an' made him walk her crost the porch. She hedn't ben on her feet fer more'n a minute fer ten months an' 'twas more'n she could stan'. She was jest as bright an' happy all thet day, an' when he went 'way she waved her hand as happy like an' smiled an' said she was glad to be able to send him back to his work. But she never said a word about his comin' back. He kep' sayin' he would come back next spring, but she only smiled, an' tole him he might not be able to leave his work, an' 'twas all right. She wanted him to be faithful.

"Well, he went, an' the coach hedn't no more'n got down the hill an' up again an' out o' sight behind the bridge 'fore she calls to me an' she says, ' 'Meelia Ellen, I believe I'm tired with all the goin's on there's been, an' if you don't mind I think I'll take a nap. So I helps her into her room and fixes her into her night things an' thur she's laid ever since, an' it's six whole weeks ef it's a day. Every mornin' fer a spell I'd go in an' say 'Ain't you ready fer me to fix you fer the day,

Mis' Brownleigh?' An' she'd jest smile an' say, 'Well, I b'leeve not just now, 'Meelia Ellen. I think I'll just rest to-day yet. Maybe I'll feel stronger to-morrow'; but to-morrow never comes, an' it's my thinkin' she'll never git up agin.''

The tears were streaming down the good woman's cheeks now and Hazel's eyes were bright with tears too. She had noticed the transparency of the delicate flesh, the frailness of the wrinkled hands. The woman's words brought conviction to her heart also.

"What does the doctor say?'' she asked, catching at a hope.

"Well, he ain't much fer talk,'' said Amelia Ellen lifting her tear-stained face from her gingham apron where it had been bowed. "It seems like them two hev just got a secret between 'em thet they won't say nothin' 'bout it. Seems like he understands, and knows she don't want folks to talk about it nor worry 'bout her.''

"But her son—'' faltered Hazel. "He ought to be told!''

"Yes, but 'tain't no use; she won't let yeh. I ast her oncet didn't she want me to write him to come an' make her a little visit just to chirk her up, and she shook her head and looked real frightened, and she says: ' 'Meelia Ellen, don't you never go to sendin' fer him 'thout lettin' me know. I should *not* like it *'tall*. He's out there doin' his work, an' I'm happier havin' him at it. A missionary can't take time traipsin' round the country every time a relative gets a little down. I'm jest perfectly all right, 'Meelia Ellen, only I went pretty hard durin' 'Sembly week, and when John was here, an' I'm restin' up fer a while. If I want John sent fer I'll tell you, but *don't you go to doin' it 'fore!*' An' I really b'leeve she'd be mad at me if I did. She lots a good deal on givin' her son, an' it would sort o' spoil her sakkerfize, I s'pose, to hev him come back every time she hungers fer him. I b'leeve in my heart she's plannin' to slip away quiet and not bother him to say good-bye. It jest looks thet way to me.''

But the next few days the invalid brightened perceptibly, and Hazel began to be reassured. Sweet converse they had together, and the girl heard the long pleasant story of the son's visit home as the mother dwelt lovingly upon each detail, telling it over and over, until the listener felt that every spot within sight of the invalid's window was fragrant with his memory. She enjoyed the tale as much as the teller, and knew just how to give the answer that one loving woman wants from another loving woman when they speak of the beloved.

Then when the story all was told over and over and there was nothing more to tell except the pleasant recalling of a funny speech, or some tender happening, Hazel began to ask deeper questions about the things of life and eternity; and step by step the older woman led her in the path she had led her son through all the years of his childhood.

During this time she seemed to grow stronger again. There were days when she sat up for a little while, and let them put the meals on a tiny swinging table by her chair; and she took a deep interest in leading the girl to a heavenly knowledge. Every day she asked for her writing materials and wrote for a little while; yet Hazel noticed that she did not send all that she had written in the envelope of the weekly letters, but laid it away carefully in her writing portfolio as if it were something yet unfinished.

And one evening in late September, when the last rays of the sunset were lying across the foot of the wheeled chair, and Amelia Ellen was building a bit of a fire in the fireplace because it seemed chilly, the mother called Hazel to her and handed her a letter sealed and addressed to her son.

"Dear," she said gently, "I want you to take this letter and put it away carefully and keep it until I am gone, and then I want you to promise that, if possible for you to do it, you will give it to my son with your own hands."

Hazel took the letter reverently, her heart filled with awe and sorrow and stooped anxiously over her friend. "Oh, why"—she cried—"what is the matter? Do you feel worse to-night? You have seemed so bright all day."

"Not a bit," said the invalid cheerily. "But I have been writing this for a long time—a sort of good-bye to my boy—and there is nobody in the world I would like to have give it to him as well as you. Will it trouble you to promise me, my dear?"

Hazel with kisses and tears protested that she would be glad to fulfill the mission, but begged that she might be allowed to send for the beloved son at once, for a sight of his face, she knew, would be good to his mother.

At last her fears were allayed, though she was by no means sure that the son ought not to be sent for, and when the invalid was happily gone to sleep, Hazel went to her room and tried to think how she might write a letter that would not alarm the young man, while yet it would bring him to his mother's side. She planned how she would go away herself for a few days, so that he need not find her here. She wrote several stiff little notes but none of them satisfied her. Her heart longed to write: "Oh, my dear! Come quickly, for your beloved mother needs you. Come, for my heart is crying out for the sight of you! Come at once!" But finally before she slept she sealed and addressed a dignified letter from Miss Radcliffe, his mother's trained nurse, suggesting that he make at least a brief visit at this time as she must be away for a few days, and she felt that his presence would be a wise thing. His mother did not seem so well as when he was with her. Then she lay down comforted to sleep. But the letter was never sent.

In the early dawn of the morning, when the faithful Amelia Ellen slipped from her couch in the alcove just off the invalid's room, and went to touch a match to the carefully laid fire in the fireplace, she passed the bed and, as had been her custom for years, glanced to see if all was well with her patient; at once she knew that the sweet spirit of the mother had fled.

With her face slightly turned away, a smile of good-night upon her lips, and the peace of God upon her brow, the mother had entered into her rest.

XIII

The Call of the Desert

Hazel, with her eyes blinded with tears and her heart swelling with the loss of the woman upon whose motherliness she had come to feel a claim, burned the letter she had written the night before, and sent a carefully worded telegram, her heart yearning with sympathy towards the bereaved son.

"Your dear mother has gone home, quietly, in her sleep. She did not seem any worse than usual, and her last words were of you. Let us know at once what plans we shall make. Nurse Radcliffe." That was the telegram she sent.

Poor Amelia Ellen was all broken up. Her practical common sense for once had fled her. She would do nothing but weep and moan for the beloved invalid whom she had served so long and faithfully. It fell to Hazel to make all decisions, though the neighbours and old friends were most kind with offers of help. Hazel waited anxiously for an answer to the telegram, but night fell and no answer had come. There had been a storm and something was wrong with the wires. The next morning, however, she sent another telegram, and about noon still a third, with as yet no response. She thought perhaps he had not waited to telegraph but had started immediately, and might be with them in a few hours. She watched the evening stage, but he did not come; then realized how her heart was in a flutter, and wondered how she would have had strength to meet him had he come. There was the letter from his mother, and her promise. She had that excuse for her presence—of course she could not have left under the circumstances. Yet she shrank from the meeting, for it seemed somehow a breach of etiquette that she should be the one to break the separation that he had chosen should be between them.

However, he did not come, and the third morning, when it

became imperative that something definite should be known, a telegram to the station agent in Arizona brought answer that the missionary was away on a long trip among some tribes of Indians; that his exact whereabouts was not known, but messengers had been sent after him, and word would be sent as soon as possible. The minister and the old neighbours advised with Amelia Ellen and Hazel, and made simple plans for the funeral, yet hoped and delayed as long as possible, and when at last after repeated telegrams there still came the answer, "Messenger not yet returned," they bore the worn-out body of the woman to a quiet resting place beside her beloved husband in the churchyard on the hillside where the soft maples scattered bright covering over the new mound, and the sky arched high with a kind of triumphant reminder of where the spirit was gone.

Hazel tried to have every detail just as she thought he would have liked it. The neighbours brought of their homely flowers in great quantities, and some city friends who had been old summer boarders sent hot-house roses. The minister conducted the beautiful service of faith, and the village children sang about the casket of their old friend, who had always loved every one of them, their hands full of the late flowers from her own garden, bright scarlet and blue and gold, as though it were a joyous occasion. Indeed, Hazel had the impression, even as she moved in the hush of the presence of death, that she was helping at some solemn festivity of deep joy instead of a funeral—so glorious had been the hope of the one who was gone, so triumphant her faith in her Saviour.

After the funeral was over Hazel sat down and wrote a letter telling about it all, filling it with sympathy, trying to show their effort to have things as he would have liked them, and expressing deep sorrow that they had been compelled to go on with the service without him.

That night there came a message from the Arizona station agent. The missionary had been found in a distant Indian hogan with a dislocated ankle. He sent word that they must not wait for him; that he would get there in time, if possible. A later message the next day said he was still unable to travel, but would get to the railroad as soon as possible. Then came an interval of several days without any word from Arizona.

Hazel went about with Amelia Ellen, putting the house in order, hearing the beautiful plaint of the loving-hearted, mourning servant as she told little incidents of her mistress. Here was the chair she sat in the last time she went up-stairs to oversee the spring regulating, and that was Mr. John's little baby dress in which he was christened. His mother smoothed it out and told her the story of his baby loveliness one day. She had laid it away herself in the box with the blue shoes and the crocheted cap. It was the last time she ever came up-stairs.

There was the gray silk dress she wore to weddings and dinner parties before her husband died, and beneath it in the trunk was the white embroidered muslin that was her wedding gown. Yellow with age it was, and delicate as a spider's web, with frostwork of yellowed broidery strewn quaintly on its ancient form, and a touch of real lace. Hazel laid a reverent hand on the fine old fabric, and felt, as she looked through the treasures of the old trunk, that an inner sanctuary of sweetness had been opened for her glimpsing.

At last a letter came from the West.

It was addressed to "Miss Radcliffe, Nurse," in Brownleigh's firm, clear hand, and began: "Dear madam." Hazel's hand trembled as she opened it, and the "dear madam" brought the tears to her eyes; but then, of course, he did not know.

He thanked her, with all the kindliness and courtliness of his mother's son, for her attendance on his dear mother, and told her of many pleasant things his mother had written of her ministrations. He spoke briefly of his being laid up lamed in the Indian reservation and his deep grief that he had been unable to come East to be beside his mother during her last hours, but went on to say that it had been his mother's wish, many times expressed, that he should not leave his post to come to her and that there need be "no sadness of fare well" when she "embarked," and that though it was hard for him he knew it was a fulfillment of his mother's desires. And now that she was gone, and the last look upon her dear face was impossible, he had decided that he could not bear it just yet to come home and see all the dear familiar places with her face

116

gone. He would wait a little while, until he had grown used to the thought of her in heaven, and then it would not be so hard. Perhaps he would not come home until next spring, unless something called him; he could not tell. And in any case, his injured ankle prevented him making the journey at present, no matter how much he may desire to do so. Miss Radcliffe's letter had told him that everything had been done just as he would have had it done. There was nothing further to make it a necessity that he should come. He had written to his mother's lawyer to arrange his mother's few business affairs, and it only remained for him to express his deep gratitude towards those who had stood by his dear mother when it had been made impossible for him to do so. He closed with a request that the nurse would give him her permanent address that he might be sure to find her when he found it possible to come East again, as he would enjoy thanking her face to face for what she had been to his mother.

That was all.

Hazel felt a blank dizziness settle down over her as she finished the letter. It put him miles away from her again, with years perhaps before another sight of him. She suddenly seemed fearfully alone in a world that no longer interested her. Where should she go; what do with her life now? Back to the hard grind of the hospital with nobody to care, and the heartrending scenes and tragedies that were daily enacted? Somehow her strength seemed to go from her at the thought. Here, too, she had failed. She was not fit for the life, and the hospital people had discovered it and sent her away to nurse her friend and try to get well. They had been kind and talked about when she should return to them, but she knew in her heart they felt her unfit and did not want her back.

Should she go back to her home, summon her brother and aunt, and plunge into society again? The very idea sickened her. Never again would she care for that life, she was certain. As she searched her heart to see what it was she really craved, if anything in the whole wide world, she found her only interest was in the mission field of Arizona, and now that her dear friend was gone she was cut off from knowing anything much about that.

She gathered herself together after a while and told Amelia Ellen of the decision of Mr. Brownleigh, and together they planned how the house should be closed, and everything put in order to await its master's will to return. But that night Hazel could not sleep, for suddenly, in the midst of her sad reflections, came the thought of the letter that was left in her trust.

It had been forgotten during the strenuous days that had followed the death of its writer. Hazel had thought of it only once, and that on the first morning, with a kind of comforting reflection that it would help the son to bear his sorrow, and she was glad that it was her privilege to put it into his hand. Then the perplexities of the occasion had driven it from her thoughts. Now it came back like a swift light in a dark place. There was yet the letter which she must give him. It was a precious bond that would hold him to her for a little while longer. But how should she give it to him?

Should she send it by mail? No, for that would not be fulfilling the letter of her promise. She knew the mother wished her to give it to him herself. Well, then, should she write and summon him to his old home at once, tell him of the letter and yet refuse to send it to him? How strange that would seem! How could she explain it to him? His mother's whim might be sacred to him—would be, of course—but he would think it strange that a young woman should make so much of it as not to trust the letter to the mail now that the circumstances made it impossible for him to come on at once.

Neither would it do for her to keep the letter until such a time as he should see fit to return to the East and look her up. It might be years.

The puzzling question kept whirling itself about in her mind for hours until at last she formulated a plan which seemed to solve the problem.

The plan was this. She would coax Amelia Ellen to take a trip to California with her, and on the way they would stop in Arizona and give the letter into the hands of the young man. By that time no doubt his injured ankle would be sufficiently strong to allow his return from the journey to the Indian reservation. She would say that she was going West and, as she had promised his mother she would put the letter into his hands, she had taken this opportunity to stop off and keep her promise. The trip would be a good thing for Amelia Ellen too, and take her mind off her loneliness for the mistress who was gone.

Eagerly she broached the subject to Amelia Ellen the next morning, and was met with a blank face of dismay.

"I couldn't noways you'd fix it, my dearie," she said sadly shaking her head. "I'd like nuthin' better'n to see them big trees out in Californy I've been hearin' 'bout all my life; an' summer an' winter with snow on the mountains what some of the boarders 't the inn tells 'bout; but I can bring it 'bout. You see it's this way. Peter Burley 'n' I ben promused fer nigh on to twelve year now, an' when he ast me I said no, I couldn't leave Mis' Brownleigh long's she needed me; an' he sez will I marry him the week after she dies, an' I sez I didn't like no sech dismal way o' puttin' it; an' he sez well, then, will I marry him the week after she don't need me no more; an' I sez yes, I will, an' now I gotta keep my promus! I can't go back on my faithful word. I'd like real well to see them big trees, but I gotta keep my promus! You see he's waited long 'nough, an' he's ben real patient. Not always he cud get to see me every week, an' he might 'a' tuk Delmira that cooked to the inn five year ago. She'd 'a' had him in a minnit, an' she done her best to git him, but he stayed faithful, an' he sez, sez he, ' 'Meelia El'n, ef you're meanin' to keep your word, I'll wait ef it's a lifetime, but I hope you won't make it any longer'n you need;' an' the night he said that I promused him agin I'd be hisn soon ez ever I was free to do's I pleased. I'd like to see them big trees, but I can't do it. I jes' can't do it."

Now Hazel was not a young woman who was easily balked in her plans when once they were made. She was convinced that the only thing to do was to take this trip and that Amelia Ellen was the only person in the world she wanted for a companion; therefore she made immediate acquaintance with Peter Burley, a heavy-browed, thoughtful, stolid man, who looked his character of patient lover, every inch of him, blue overalls and all. Hazel's heart almost misgave her as she unfolded her plan to his astonished ears, and saw the look of blank dismay that overspread his face. However, he had not waited all these years to refuse his sweetheart anything in reason now. He drew a deep sigh, inquired how long the trip as planned would take, allowed he "could wait another month ef that would suit,'' and turned patiently to his barn-yard to think his weary thoughts, and set his hopes a little further ahead. Then Hazel's heart misgave her. She called after him and suggested that perhaps he might like to have the marriage first and go with them, taking the excursion as a wedding trip. She would gladly pay all expenses if he would. But the man shook his head.

"I couldn't leave the stock fer that long, ennyhow you fix it. Thur ain't no one would know to take my place. Besides, I never was fer takin' journeys; but 'Meelia Ellen, she's allus ben of a sprightlier disposition, an' ef she hez a hankerin' after Californy, I 'spect she'll be kinder more contended like ef she sees 'em first an' then settles down in Granville. She better go while she's got the chancet.''

Amelia Ellen succumbed, albeit with tears. Hazel could not tell whether she was more glad or sad at the prospect before her. Whiles Amelia Ellen wept and bemoaned the fate of poor Burley, and whiles she questioned whether there really were any big trees like what you saw in the geographies with riding parties sitting contentedly in tunnels through their trunks. But at last she consented to go, and with many an injunction from the admiring and envious neighbours who came to see them off, Amelia Ellen bade a sobbing good-bye to her solemn lover in the gray dawn of an October morning, climbed into the stage beside Hazel, and they drove away into the mystery of the great world. As she looked back at her Peter, standing patient, stooped and gray in the familiar village street, look-ing after his departing sweetheart who was going out sightsee-ing into the world, Amelia Ellen would almost have jumped out over the wheel and run back if it had not been for what the neighbours would say, for her heart was Burley's; and now that the big trees were actually pulling harder than Burley, and she had decided to go and see them, Burley began by his very acquiescence to pull harder than the big trees. It was a very teary Amelia Ellen who climbed into the train a few hours later, looking back dismally, hopelessly, towards the old stage they had just left, and wondering after all if she ever would get back to Granville safe and alive again. Strange fears visited her of dangers that might come to Burley during her absence, which if they did she would never forgive herself for having left him; strange horrors of the way of things that might hinder her return; and she began to regard her hitherto beloved travelling companion with almost suspicion, as if she were a conspirator against her welfare.

However, as the miles grew and the wonders of the way multiplied, Amelia Ellen began to sit up and take notice, and to have a sort of excited exultance that she had come; for were they not nearing the great famed West now, and would it not soon be time to see the big trees and turn back home again? She was almost glad she had come. She would be wholly glad she had done so when she had got back safely home once more.

And so one evening about sunset they arrived at the little station in Arizona which over a year ago Hazel had left in her father's private car.

XIV
Home

Amelia Ellen, stiff from the unaccustomed travel, powdered with the dust of the desert, wearied with the excitement of travel and lack of sleep amid her strange surroundings, stepped down upon the wooden platform and surveyed the magnificent distance between herself and anywhere; observed the vast emptiness, with awful purpling mountains and limitless stretches of vari-coloured ground arched by a dome of sky, higher and wider and more dazzling than her stern New Hampshire soul had ever conceived, and turned panic-stricken back to the train which was already moving away from the little station. Her first sensation had been one of relief at feeling solid ground under her feet once more, for this was the first trip into the world Amelia Ellen had ever made, and the cars bewildered her. Her second impulse was to get back into that train as fast as her feet could carry her and get this awful journey done so that she might earn the right to return to her quiet home and her faithful lover.

But the train was well under way. She looked after it half in envy. It could go on with its work and not have to stop in this wild waste.

She gazed about again with the frightened look a child deserted gives before it puckers its lips and screams.

Hazel was talking composedly with the rough-looking man on the platform, who wore a wide felt hat and a pistol in his belt. He didn't look even respectable to Amelia Ellen's provincial eyes. And behind him, horror of horrors! loomed a real live Indian, long hair, high cheek bones, blanket and all, just as she had seen them in the geography! Her blood ran cold! Why, oh why, had she ever been left to do this daring thing—to leave civilization and come away from her good man and the quiet home awaiting her to certain death in the desert. All the stories of horrid scalpings she had ever heard appeared before her excited vision. With a gasp she turned again to the departing train, which had become a mere speck on the desert, and even as she looked vanished around a curve and was lost in the dim foot-hills of a mountain!

Poor Amelia Ellen! Her head reeled and her heart sank. The vast prairie engulfed her, as it were, and she stood trembling and staring in dazed expectancy of an attack from earth or air or sky. The very sky and ground seemed tottering together and threatening to extinguish her, and she closed her eyes, caught her breath and prayed for Peter. It had been her habit always in any emergency to pray for Peter Burley.

It was no better when they took her to the eating-house across the track. She picked her way among the evil-looking men, and surveyed the long dining table with its burden of coarse food and its board seats with disdain, declined to take off her hat when she reached the room to which the slatternly woman showed them because she said there was no place to lay it down that was fit; scorned the simple bed, refused to wash her hands at the basin furnished for all, and made herself more disagreeable than Hazel had dreamed her gentle, serviceable Amelia Ellen ever could have been. No supper would she eat, nor would she remain long at the table after the men began to file in, with curious eyes towards the strangers.

She stalked to the rough, unroofed porch in the front and stared off at the dark vastness, afraid of the wild strangeness, afraid of the looming mountains, afraid of the multitude of stars. She said it was ridiculous to have so many stars. It wasn't natural. It was irreverent. It was like looking too close into heaven when you weren't intended to.

And then a blood-curdling sound arose! It made her very hair stand on end. She turned with wild eyes and grasped Hazel's arm, but she was too frightened to utter a sound. Hazel had just come out to sit with her. The men out of deference to the strangers had withdrawn from their customary smoking place on the porch to the back of the wood-pile behind the house. They were alone—the two women—out there in the dark, with that awful, awful sound!

Amelia Ellen's white lips framed the words "Indians"?

"War-whoop"? but her throat refused her sound and her breath came short.

"Coyotes!" laughed Hazel, secure in her wide experience, with almost a joyous ring to her voice. The sound of those distant beasts assured her that she was in the land of her beloved at last and her soul rejoiced.

"Coy—oh——" but Amelia Ellen's voice was lost in the recesses of her skimpy pillow whither she had fled to bury her startled ears. She had heard of coyotes, but she had never imagined to hear one outside of a zoölogical garden, of which she had read and always hoped one day to visit. There she lay on her hard little bed and quaked until Hazel, laughing still, came to find her; but all she could get from the poor soul was a pitiful plaint about Burley. "And what would he say if I was to be et with one of them creatures? He'd never forgive me, never, never s'long's I lived! I hadn't ough' to 'a' come. I hadn't ough' to 'a' come!"

Nothing Hazel could say would allay her fears. She listened with horror as the girl attempted to show how harmless the beasts were by telling of her own night ride up the canyon, and how nothing harmed her. Amelia Ellen merely looked at her with frozen glance made fiercer by the flickering candle flare, and answered dully: "An' you knew 'bout 'em all 'long, an' yet you brung me! It ain't what I thought you'd do! Burley, he'll never fergive me s'long's I live ef I get et up. It ain't ez if I was all alone in the world, you know. I got him to think of an' I can't afford to run no resks of bein' et, *ef you can*."

Not a wink of sleep did she get that night and when the morning dawned and to the horrors of the night were added a telegram from a neighbour of Burley's saying that Burley had fallen from the haymow and broken his leg, but he sent his respects and hoped they'd have a good journey, Amelia Ellen grew uncontrollable. She declared she would not stay in that awful country another minute. That she would take the first train back—back to her beloved New Hampshire which she never again would leave so long as her life was spared, unless Burley went along. She would not even wait until Hazel had delivered her message. How could two lone women deliver a message in a land like that? Never, *never* would she ride, drive or walk, no, nor even set foot on the sand of the desert.

124

She would sit by the track until a train came along and she would not even look further than she need. The frenzy of fear which sometimes possesses simple people at sight of a great body of water, or a roaring torrent pouring over a precipice, had taken possession of her at sight of the desert. It filled her soul with its immensity, and poor Amelia Ellen had a great desire to sit down on the wooden platform and grasp firm hold of something until a train came to rescue her from this awful emptiness which had tried to swallow her up.

Poor Peter, with his broken leg, was her weird cry! One would think she had broken it with the wheels of the car in which she had travelled away from him by the way she took on about it and blamed herself. The tragedy of a broken vow and its consequences was the subject of her discourse. Hazel laughed, then argued, and finally cried and besought; but nothing could avail. Go she would, and that speedily, back to her home.

When it became evident that arguments and tears were of no use and that Amelia Ellen was determined to go home with or without her, Hazel withdrew to the front porch and took counsel with the desert in its morning brightness, with the purple luring mountains, and the smiling sky. Go back on the train that would stop at the station in half an hour, with the desert there, and the wonderful land, and its strange, wistful people, and not even see a glimpse of him she loved? Go back with the letter still in her possession and her message still ungiven? Never! Surely she was not afraid to stay long enough to send for him. The woman who had fed them and sheltered them for the night would be her protector. She would stay. There must be some woman of refinement and culture somewhere near by to whom she could go for a few days until her errand was performed; and what was her training in the hospital worth if it did not give her some independence? Out here in the wild free West women had to protect themselves. She could surely stay in the uncomfortable quarters where she was for another day until she could get word to the missionary. Then she could decide whether to proceed on her journey alone to California, or to go back home. There was really no reason why she should not travel alone if she chose; plenty of young women did and, anyway, the emergency was not of her choosing. Amelia Ellen would make herself sick fretting over her Burley, that was plain, if she were detained even a few hours. Hazel came back to the nearly demented Amelia Ellen with her chin tilted firmly and a straight little set of her sweet lips which betokened stubbornness. The train came in a brief space of time, and, weeping but firm, Amelia Ellen boarded it, dismayed at the thought of leaving her dear young lady, yet stubbornly determined to go. Hazel gave her the ticket and plenty of money, charged the conductor to look after her, waved a brave farewell and turned back to the desert alone.

A brief conference with the woman who had entertained them, who was also the wife of the station agent, brought out the fact that the missionary was not yet returned from his journey, but a message received from him a few days before spoke of his probable return on the morrow or the day after. The woman advised that the lady go to the fort where visitors were always welcomed and where there were luxuries more fitted to the stranger's habit. She eyed the dainty apparel of her guest enviously as she spoke, and Hazel, keenly alive to the meaning of her look, realized that the woman, like the missionary, had judged her unfit for life in the desert. She was half determined to stay where she was until the missionary's return, and show that she could adapt herself to any surroundings, but she saw that the woman was anxious to have her gone. It probably put her out to have a guest of another world than her own.

The woman told her that a trusty Indian messenger was here from the fort and was riding back soon. If the lady cared she could get a horse and go under his escort. She opened her eyes in wonder when Hazel asked if there was to be a woman in the party, and whether she could not leave her work for a little while and ride over with them if she would pay her well for the service.

"Oh, you needn't bring none o' them fine lady airs out here!" she declared rudely. "We-all ain't got time fer no sech foolery. You needn't be afraid to go back with Joe. He takes care of the women at the fort. He'll look after you fine. You'll mebbe kin hire a horse to ride, an' strop yer baggage on. Yer trunk ye kin leave here."

Hazel, half frightened at the position she had allowed herself to be placed in, considered the woman's words, and when she had looked upon the Indian's stolid countenance decided to accept his escort. He was an old man with furrowed face and sad eyes that looked as if they could tell great secrets, but there was that in his face that made her trust him, she knew not why.

An hour later, her most necessary baggage strapped to the back of the saddle on a wicked-looking little pony, Hazel, with a sense of deep excitement, mounted and rode away behind the solemn, silent Indian. She was going to the fort to ask shelter, until her errand was accomplished, of the only women in that region who would be likely to take her in. She had a feeling that the thing she was doing was a most wild and unconventional proceeding and would come under the grave condemnation of her aunt, and all her New York friends. She was most thankful that they were far away and could not interfere, for somehow she felt that she must do it anyway. She must put that letter, with her own hands, into the possession of its owner.

It was a most glorious morning. The earth and the heavens seemed newly made for the day. Hazel felt a gladness in her soul that would not down, even when she thought of poor Amelia Ellen crouched in her corner of the sleeper, miserable at her desertion, yet determined to go. She thought of the dear mother, and wondered if 'twere given to her to know now how she was trying to fulfill her last wish. It was pleasant to think she knew and was glad, and Hazel felt as though her presence was near and protecting her.

The silent Indian made few remarks. He rode ahead always with a grave, thoughful expression, like a student whose thoughts are not to be disturbed. He nodded gravely in answer to the questions Hazel asked him whenever they stopped to water the horses, but he volunteered no information beyond calling her attention to a lame foot her pony was developing.

Several times Joe got down and examined the pony's foot, and shook his head, with a grunt of worried disapproval. Presently as the miles went by Hazel began to notice the pony's lameness herself, and became alarmed lest he would break down altogether in the midst of the desert. Then what would the Indian do? Certainly not give her his horse and foot it, as the missionary had done. She could not expect that every man in this desert was like the one who had cared for her before. What a foolish girl she had been to get herself into this fix! And now there was no father to send out search parties for her, and no missionary at home to find her!

The dust, the growing heat of the day, and the anxiety began to wear upon her. She was tired and hungry, and when at noon the Indian dismounted beside a water-hole where the water tasted of sheep who had passed through but a short time before, and handed her a package of corn bread and cold bacon, while he withdrew to the company of the horses for his own siesta, she was feign to put her head down on the coarse grass and weep for her folly in coming out to this wild country alone, or at least in being so headstrong as to stay when Amelia Ellen deserted her. Then the thought suddenly occurred to her: how would Amelia Ellen have figured in this morning's journey on horseback; and instead of weeping she fell to laughing almost hysterically.

She munched the corn bread—the bacon she could not eat—and wondered if the woman at the stopping-place had realized what an impossible lunch she had provided for her guest. However, here was one of the tests. She was not worth much if a little thing like coarse food annoyed her so much. She drank some of the bitter water, and bravely ate a second piece of corn bread and tried to hope her pony would be all right after his rest. But it was evident after they had gone a mile or two further that the pony was growing worse. He lagged, and limped, and stopped, and it seemed almost cruel to urge him further, yet what could be done? The Indian rode behind now, watching him and speaking in low grunts to him occasionally, and finally they came in sight of a speck of a building in the distance. Then the Indian spoke. Pointing towards the distant building, which seemed too tiny for human habitation, he said: "Aneshodi hogan. Him friend me. Lady stay. Me come back good horse. Pony no go more. He bad!"

Dismay filled the heart of the lady. She gathered that her guide wished to leave her by the way while he went on for another horse, and maybe he would return and maybe not. Meantime, what kind of a place was he leaving her in? Would there be a woman there? Even if she were an Indian woman that would not be so bad. "Aneshodi" sounded as if it might be a woman's name.

"Is this Aneshodi a woman?" she questioned.

The Indian shook his head and grunted. "Na, na. Aneshodi, Aneshodi. Him friend me. Him good friend. No woman!" (In scorn.)

"Is there no woman in the house?" she asked anxiously.

"Na! Him heap good man. Good hogan. Lady stay. Rest."

Suddenly her pony stumbled and nearly fell. She saw that she could not depend on him for long now.

"Couldn't I walk with you?" she asked, her eyes pleading. "I would rather walk than stay. Is it far?"

The Indian shook his head vigorously.

"Lady no walk. Many suns lady walk. Great mile. Lady stay. Me ride fast. Back sundown," and he pointed to the sun which was even now beginning its downward course.

Hazel saw there was nothing for it but to do as the Indian said, and indeed his words seemed reasonable, but she was very much frightened. What kind of a place was this in which she was to stay? As they neared it appeared to be nothing but a little weather-beaten shanty, with a curiously familiar look, as if she had passed that way before. A few chickens were picking about the yard, and a vine grew over the door, but there was no sign of human being about and the desert stretched wide and barren on every side. Her old fear of its vastness returned, and she began to have a fellow feeling with Amelia Ellen. She saw now that she ought to have gone with Amelia Ellen back to civilization and found somebody who would have come with her on her errand. But then the letter would have been longer delayed!

The thought of the letter kept up her courage, and she descended dubiously from her pony's back, and followed the Indian to the door of the shanty. The vine growing luxuriantly over window and casement and door frame reassured her somewhat, she could not tell just why. Perhaps somebody with a sense of beauty lived in the ugly little building, and a man with a sense of beauty could not be wholly bad. But how was she to stay alone in a man's house where no woman lived? Perhaps the man would have a horse to lend or sell them. She would offer any sum he wanted if she only could get to a safe place.

But the Indian did not knock at the door as she had expected he would do. Instead he stooped to the lower step, and putting his hand into a small opening in the woodwork of the step, fumbled there a minute and presently brought out a key which he fitted into the lock and threw the door wide open to her astonished gaze.

"Him friend me!" explained the Indian again.

He walked into the room with the manner of a partial proprietor of the place, looked about, stooped down to the fireplace where a fire was neatly laid, and set it blazing up cheerfully; took the water bucket and filled it, and putting some water into the kettle swung it over the blaze to heat, then turning he spoke again:

"Lady stay. Me come back—soon. Sun no go down. Me come back; good horse get lady."

"But where is the owner of this house? What will he think of my being here when he comes back?" said Hazel, more frightened than ever at the prospect of being left. She had not expected to stay entirely alone. She had counted on finding some one in the house.

"Aneshodi way off. Not come back one—two—day mebbe! He know me. He me friend. Lady stay! All right!"

Hazel, her eyes large with fear, watched her protector mount and ride away. Almost she called after him that he must not leave her; then she remembered that this was a part of a woman's life in Arizona, and she was being tried. It was just such things as this the missionary had meant when he said she was unfit for life out here. She would stay and bear the loneliness and fright. She would prove, at least to herself, that she had the courage of any missionary. She would not bear the ignominy of weakness and failure. It would be a shame to her all her life to know she had failed in this trying time.

She watched the Indian riding rapidly away as if he were in hot haste. Once the suspicion crossed her mind that perhaps he had lamed her horse on purpose, and left her here just to get rid of her. Perhaps this was the home of some dreadful person who would return soon and do her harm.

She turned quickly, with alarm in her heart, to see what manner of place she was in, for she had been too excited at first over the prospect of being left to notice it much, save to be surprised that there were chairs, a fireplace, and a look of comparative comfort. Now she looked about to find out if possible just what sort of a person the owner might be, and glancing at the table near the fireplace the first object her eye fell upon was an open book, and the words that caught her vision were: "He that dwelleth in the secret place of the Most High shall abide under the shadow of the Almighty!"

With a start she turned the book over and found it was a Bible, bound in plain, strong covers, with large, clear print, and it lay open as if the owner had been reading it but a short time before and had been called suddenly away.

With a sigh of relief she sank down in the big chair by the fire and let the excited tears have their way. Somehow her fear all vanished with that sentence. The owner of the house could not be very bad when he kept his Bible about and open to that psalm, her psalm, her missionary's psalm! And there was assurance in the very words themselves, as if they had been sent to remind her of her new trust in an Unseen Power. If she was making the Most High her dwelling place continually, surely she was under His protection continually, and had no need to be afraid anywhere, for she was abiding in Him. The thought gave her a strange new sense of sweetness and safety.

After a moment she sat up wiping away the tears and began to look around. Perhaps this was the home of some friend of her missionary. She felt comforted about staying here now. She lifted her eyes to the wall above the mantel and lo, there smiled the face of her dear friend, the mother, who had just gone home to heaven, and beneath it—as if that were not enough to bring a throb of understanding and joy to her heart—beneath it hung her own little jewelled riding whip which she had left on the desert a year ago and forgotten.

Suddenly, with a cry of joy, she rose and clasped her hands over her heart, relief and happiness in every line of her face.

"It is his home! I have come to his own house!" she cried and looked about her with the joy of discovery. This then was where he lived—there were his books, here his chair where he sat and rested or studied—his hands had left the Bible open at her psalm, his psalm—*their* psalm! There was his couch over behind the screen, and at the other end the tiny table and the dishes in the closet! Everything was in place, and careful neatness reigned, albeit an air of manlike uncertainty about some things.

She went from one end to the other of the big room and

back again, studying every detail, revelling in the thought that now, whatever came to her, she might take back with her a picture of himself in his own quiet room when his work was laid aside for a little, and when, if ever he had time and allowed himself, he perhaps thought of her.

Time flew on winged feet. With the dear face of her old friend smiling down upon her and that psalm open beside her on the table, she never thought of fear. And presently she remembered she was hungry, and went foraging in the cupboard for something to eat. She found plenty of supplies, and after she had satisfied her hunger sat down in the great chair by the fire and looked about her in contentment. With the peace of the room, his room, upon her, and the sweet old face from the picture looking down in benediction as if in welcome, she felt happier than since her father had died.

The quiet of the desert afternoon brooded outside, the fire burned softly lower and lower at her side, the sun bent down to the west, and long rays stole through the window and across at her feet, but the golden head was drooping and the long-lashed eyes were closed. She was asleep in his chair. and the dying firelight played over her face.

Then, quietly, without any warning, the door opened and a man walked into the room!

XV

The Way Of The Cross

The missionary had been a far journey to an isolated tribe of Indians outside his own reservation. It was his first visit to them since the journey he had taken with his colleague, and of which he had told Hazel during their companionship in the desert. He had thought to go sooner, but matters in his own extended parish, and his trip East, had united to prevent him.

They had lain upon his heart, these lonely, isolated people of another age, living amid the past in their ancient houses high up on the cliffs; a little handful of lonely, primitive children, existing afar; knowing nothing of God and little of man; with their strange, simple ways, and their weird appearance. They had come to him in visions as he prayed, and always with a weight upon his soul as of a message undelivered.

He had taken his first opportunity after his return from the East to go to them; but it had not been as soon as he had hoped. Matters in connection with the new church had demanded his attention, and then when they were arranged satisfactorily one of his flock was smitten with a lingering illness, and so hung upon his friendship and companionship that he could not with a clear conscience go far away. But at last all hindrances subsided and he went forth on his mission.

The Indians had received him gladly, noting his approach from afar and coming down the steep way to meet him, putting their rude best at his disposal, and opening their hearts to him. No white man had visited them since his last coming with his friend, save a trader who had lost his way, and who knew little about the God of whom the missionary had spoken, or the Book of Heaven; at least he had not seemed to understand. Of these things he was as ignorant, perhaps, as they.

The missionary entered into the strange family life of the

tribe who inhabited the vast, many-roomed palace of rock carved high at the top of the cliff. He laughed with them, ate with them, slept with them, and in every way gained their full confidence. He played with their little children, teaching them many new games and amusing tricks, and praising the quick wits of the little ones; while their elders stood about, the stolid look of their dusky faces relaxed into smiles of deep interest and admiration.

And then at night he told them of the God who set the stars above them; who made the earth and them, and loved them; and of Jesus, His only Son, who came to die for them and who would not only be their Saviour, but their loving companion by day and by night; unseen, but always at hand, caring for each one of His children individually, knowing their joys and their sorrows. Gradually he made them understand that he was the servant—the messenger—of this Christ, and had come there for the express purpose of helping them to know their unseen Friend. Around the camp-fire, under the starry dome, or on the sunny plain, whenever he taught them they listened, their faces losing the wild, half-animal look of the uncivilized, and taking on the hidden longing that all mortals have in common. He saw the humanity in them looking wistfully through their great eyes, and gave himself to teach them.

Sometimes as he talked he would lift his face to the sky, and close his eyes; and they would listen with awe as he spoke to his Father in heaven. They watched him at first and looked up as if they half expected to see the Unseen World open before their wondering gaze; but gradually the spirit of devotion claimed them, and they closed their eyes with him, and who shall say if the savage prayers within their breasts were not more acceptable to the Father than many a wordy petition put up in the temples of civilization?

Seven days and nights he abode with them, and they fain would have claimed him for their own, and begged him to give up all other places and live there always. They would give him of their best. He would not need to work, for they would give him his portion, and make him a home as he should direct them. In short, they would enshrine him in their hearts as a kind of undergod, representing to their childish minds the true and Only One, the knowledge of whom he had brought to them.

But he told them of his work, of why he must go back to it, and sadly they prepared to bid him good-bye with many an invitation for return. In going down the cliff, where he had gone with them many a time before, he turned to wave another farewell to a little child who had been his special pet, and turning, slipped, and wrenched his ankle so badly that he could not move on.

They carried him up to their home again, half sorrowful, but wholly triumphant. He was theirs for a little longer; and there were more stories he could tell. The Book of Heaven was a large one, and they wanted to hear it all. They spread his couch of their best, and wearied themselves to supply his necessity with all that their ignorance imagined he needed, and then they sat at his feet and listened. The sprain was a troublesome one and painful, and it yielded to treatment but slowly; meanwhile the messenger arrived with the telegram from the East.

They gathered about it, that sheet of yellow paper with its mysterious scratches upon it, which told such volumes to their friend, but gave no semblance to sign language of anything in heaven above or earth beneath. They looked with awe upon their friend as they saw the anguish in his countenance. His mother was dead! This man who had loved her, and had left her to bring them news of salvation, was suffering. It was one more bond between them, one more tie of common humanity. And yet he could look up and smile, and still speak to the invisible Father! They saw his face as it were the face of an angel with the light of the comfort of Christ upon it; and when he read to them and tried to make them understand the majestic words: "O death, where is thy sting? O grave, where is thy victory?" they sat and looked afar off, and thought of the ones that they had lost. This man said they would all live again. His mother would live; the chief they had lost last year, the bravest and youngest chief of all their tribe, he would live too; their little children would live; all they had lost would live again.

So, when he would most have wished to be alone with his God and his sorrow, he must needs lay aside his own bitter grief, and bring these childish people consolation for their griefs, and in doing so the comfort came to him also. For somehow, looking into their longing faces, and seeing their utter need, and how eagerly they hung upon his words, he came to feel the presence of the Comforter standing by his side in the dark cave shadows, whispering to his heart sweet words that he long had known but had not fully comprehended because his need for them had never come before. Somehow time and things of earth receded, and only heaven and immortal souls mattered. He was lifted above his own loss and into the joy of the inheritance of the servant of the Lord.

But the time had come, all too soon for his hosts, when he was able to go on his way; and most anxious he was to be started, longing for further news of the dear one who was gone from him. They followed him in sorrowful procession far into the plain to see him on his way, and then returned to their mesa and their cliff home to talk of it all and wonder.

Alone upon the desert at last, the three great mesas like fingers of a giant hand stretching cloudily behind him; the purpling mountains in the distance; the sunlight shining vividly down over all the bright sands; the full sense of his loss came at last upon him, and his spirit was bowed with the weight of it. The vision of the Mount was passed, and the valley of the shadow of life was upon him. It came to him what it would be to have no more of his mother's letters to cheer his loneliness; no thought of her at home thinking of him; no looking forward to another home-coming.

As he rode he saw none of the changing landscape by the way, but only the Granville orchard with its showering pink and white, and his mother lying happily beside him on the strawberry bank picking the sweet vivid berries, and smiling back to him as if she had been a girl. He was glad, glad he had that memory of her. And she had seemed so well, so very well. He had been thinking that perhaps when there was hope of building a little addition to his shack and making a possible place of comfort for her, that he might venture to propose that she come out to him and stay. It was a wish that had been growing, growing in his lonely heart since that visit home when it seemed as if he could not tear himself away from her and go back; and yet knew that he could not stay—would not want to stay, because of his beloved work. And now it was

136

over forever, his dream! She would never come to cheer his home, and he would always have to live a lonely life—for he knew in his heart there was only one girl in the whole world he would want to ask to come, and her he might not, must not ask.

As endless and as desolate as his desert his future lay stretched out before his mind. For the time his beloved work and the joy of service was sunk out of sight, and he saw only himself, alone, forsaken of all love, walking his sorrowful way apart; and there surged over him a great and deadly weakness as of a spirit in despair.

In this mind he lay down to rest in the shadow of great rock about the noon hour, too weary in spirit and exhausted in body to go further without a sleep. The faithful Billy dozed and munched his portion not far away; and high overhead a great eagle soared high and far, adding to the wide desolateness of the scene. Here he was alone at last for the first time with his grief, and for a while it had its way, and he faced it; entering into his Gethsemane with bowed spirit and seeing nothing but blackness all about him. It was so, worn with the anguish of his spirit, that he fell asleep.

While he slept there came to him peace; a dream of his mother, smiling, well, and walking with a light free step as he remembered her when he was a little boy; and by her side the girl he loved. How strange, and wonderful, that these two should come to him and bring him rest! And then, as he lay still dreaming, they smiled at him and passed on, hand in hand, the girl turning and waving her hand as if she meant to return; and presently they passed beyond his sight. The One stood by him, somewhere within the shelter of the rock under which he lay, and spoke; and the Voice thrilled his soul as it had never been thrilled in life before:

"Lo, *I* am with you *alway*, even unto the end of the world."

The Peace of that Invisible Presence descended upon him in full measure, and when he awoke he found himself repeating: "The peace which passeth understanding!" and realizing that for the first time he knew what the words meant.

Some time he lay quietly like a child who had been comforted and cared for, wondering at the burden which had been

137

lifted, glorying in the peace that had come in its place; rejoicing in the Presence that he felt would be with him always, and make it possible for him to bear the loneliness.

At last he turned his head to see if Billy were far away, and was startled to see the shadow of the rock, under which he lay, spread out upon the sand before him, the semblance of a perfect mighty cross. For so the jutting uneven arms of the rock and the position of the sun arranged the shadows before him. "The shadow of a great rock in a weary land." The words came to his memory, and it seemed to be his mother's voice repeating them as she used to do on Sabbath evenings when they sat together in the twilight before his bedtime. A weary land! It *was* a weary land now, and his soul had been parched with the heat and loneliness. He had needed the rock as he had never needed it before, and the Rock, Christ Jesus, had become a rest and a peace to his soul. But there it lay spread out upon the sand beside him, and it was the way of the cross; the Christ way was always the way of the cross. But what was the song they sang at that great meeting he attended in New York? "The way of the cross leads home." Ah, that was it. Some day it would lead him home, but now it was the way cross and he must take it with courage, and always with that unseen but close Companion who had promised to be with him even to the end of the world.

Well, he would rise up at once, strong in that blessed companionship. Cheerfully he made his preparations for starting, and now he turned Billy's head a trifle to the south, for he decided to stop over night with his colleague.

When his grief and loneliness were fresh upon him it had seemed that he could not bear this visit. But since peace had come to his soul he changed his course to take in the other mission, which was really on his way, only that he had purposely avoided it.

They made him welcome, those two who had made a little bit of earthly paradise out of their desert shack; and they compelled him to stay with them and rest three days, for he was more worn with the journey and his recent pain and sorrow than he realized. They comforted him with their loving sympathy and gladdened his soul with the sight of their own joy, albeit it gave him a feeling of being set apart from them. He started in the early dawn of the day when the morning star was yet visible, and as he rode through the beryl air of the dawning hour he was uplifted from his sadness by a sense of the near presence of Christ.

He took his way slowly, purposely turning aside three times from the trail to call at the hogans of some of his parishioners; for he dreaded the home-coming as one dreads a blow that is inevitable. His mother's picture awaited him in his own room, smiling down upon his possessions with that dear look upon her face, and to look at it for the first time knowing that she was gone from earth forever was an experience from which he shrank inexpressibly. Thus he gave himself more time, knowing that it was better to go calmly, turning his mind back to his work, and doing what she would have liked him to do.

He camped that night under the sheltered ledge where he and Hazel had been, and as he lay down to sleep he repeated the psalm they had read together that night, and felt a sense of the comfort of abiding under the shadow of the Almighty.

In visions of the night he saw the girl's face once more, and she smiled upon him with that glad welcoming look, as though she had come to be with him always. She did not say anything in the dream, but just put out her hands to him with a motion of surrender.

The vision faded as he opened his eyes, yet so real had it been that it remained with him and thrilled him with the wonder of her look all day. He began to ponder whether he had been right in persistently putting her out of his life as he had done. Bits of her own sentences came to him with new meaning and he wondered after all if he had not been a fool. Perhaps he might have won her. Perhaps God had really sent her to him to be his life companion, and he had been too blind to understand.

He put the idea from him many times with a sigh as he mended the fire and prepared his simple meal, yet always her face lingered sweetly in his thoughts, like balm upon his saddened spirit.

Billy was headed towards home that morning, and seemed eager to get on. He had not understood his master these sad days. Something had come over his spirits. The little horse neighed cheerfully and started on his way with willing gait. However lonely the master might be, home was good, with one's own stall and manger; and who might tell but some presentiment told Billy that the princess was awaiting them?

The missionary endeavoured to keep his thoughts upon his work and plans for the immediate future, but try as he would the face of 'the girl kept smiling in between; and all the beauties of the way combined to bring back the ride he had taken with her; until finally he let his fancy dwell upon her with pleasant thoughts of how it would be if she were his, and waiting for him at the end of his journey; or better still, riding beside him at this moment, bearing him sweet converse on the way.

The little shack stood silent, familiar, in the setting sunlight, as he rode up to the door and gravely arranged for Billy's comfort then with his upward look for comfort he went towards his lonely home and opening the door stood wondering upon the threshold!

XVI

The Letter

t was only an instant before she opened her eyes, for that subconscious state, that warns even in sleep of things that are going on outside the world of slumber, told her there was another soul present.

She awakened suddenly and looked up at him, the rosiness of sleep upon her cheeks and the dewiness of it upon her eyelids. She looked most adorable with the long red slant of sunset from the open door at her feet and the wonder of his coming in her face. Their eyes met, and told the story, before brain had time to give warning of danger and need of self-control.

"Oh, my darling!" the man said and took a step towards her, his arms outstretched as if he would clasp her, yet daring hardly to believe that it was really herself in the flesh.

"My darling! Have you really come to me?" He breathed the question as though its answer meant life or death to him.

She arose and stood before him, trembling with joy, abashed now that she was in his presence, in his home, unbidden. Her tongue seemed tied. She had no word with which to explain. But because he saw the love in her eyes and because his own need of her was great, he became bolder, and coming closer he began to tell her earnestly how he had longed and prayed that God would make a way for him to find her again; how he had fancied her here in this room, his own dear companion—his wife!

He breathed the word tenderly, reverently and she felt the blessing and the wonder of the love of this great simple-hearted man.

Then because he saw his answer in her eyes, he came near and took her reverently in his arms, laid his lips upon hers, and thus they stood for a moment together, knowing that after all the sorrow, the longing, the separation, each had come into his own.

It was some time before Hazel could get opportunity to explain how she came all unknowingly to be in his house, and even then he could not understand what joyful circumstance had set her face fortward and dropped her at his door. So she had to go back to the letter, the letter which was the cause of it all, and yet for the moment had been forgotten. She brought it forth now, and his face, all tender with the joy of her presence, grew almost glorified when he knew that it was she who had been his mother's tender nurse and beloved friend through the last days of her life.

With clasped hands they talked together of his mother. Hazel told him all: how she had come upon her that summer's day, and her heart had yearned to know her for his sake; and how she had gone back again, and yet again; all the story of her own struggles for a better life. When she told of her cooking lessons he kissed the little white hands he held, and when she spoke of her hospital work he touched his lips to eyes and brow in reverent worshipfulness.

"And you did all that because——?" he asked and looked deep into her eyes, demanding hungrily his answer.

"Because I wanted to be worthy of your love!" she breathed softly, her eyes down-drooped, her face rosy with her confession.

"Oh, my darling!" he said, and clasped her close once more. Almost the letter itself was forgotten, until it slipped softly to the floor and called attention to itself. There was really after all no need for the letter. It had done its intended work without being read. But they read it together, his arm about her shoulders, and their heads close, each feeling the need of the comforting love of the other because of the bereavement each had suffered.

And thus they read:

"MY DEAR SON:

"I am writing this letter in what I believe to be the last few days of my life. Long ago I made our dear doctor tell me just what would be the signs that preceded the probable culmination of my disease. He knew I would be happier so, for I had some things I wished to accomplish before I went

142

away. I did not tell you, dear son, because I knew it could but distress you and turn your thoughts away from the work to which you belong. I knew when you came home to me for that dear last visit that I had only a little while longer left here, and I need not tell you what those blessed days of your stay were to me. You know without my telling. You perhaps will blame yourself that you did not see how near the end it was and stay beside me; but John, beloved, I would not have been happy to have had it so. It would have brought before you with intensity the parting side of death, and this I wished to avoid. I want you to think of me as gone to be with Jesus and with your dear father. Besides, I wanted the pleasure of giving you back again to your work before I went away.

"It was because I knew the end was near that I dared do a lot of things that I would have been careful about otherwise. It was in the strength of the happiness of your presence that I forced myself to walk again that you might remember your mother once more on her feet. Remember now when you are reading this I shall be walking the golden streets with as strong and free a gait as you walk your desert, dear. So don't regret anything of the good time we had, nor wish you had stayed longer. It was perfect, and the good times are not over for us. We shall have them again on the other side some day when there are no more partings forever.

"But there is just one thing that has troubled me ever since you first went away, and that is that you are alone. God knew it was not good for man to be alone, and He has a helpmeet for my boy somewhere in the world, I am sure. I would be glad if I might go knowing that you had found her and that she loved you as I loved your father when I married him. I have never talked much about these things to you because I do not think mothers should try to influence their children to marry until God sends the right one, and then it is not the mother who should be the judge, of course. But once I spoke to you in a letter. You remember? It was after I had met a sweet girl whose life seemed so fitted to belong to yours. You opened your heart to me then and told me you had found the one you loved and would never love another—but she was not for you. My heart ached for you, laddie, and I prayed much for you then, for it was a sore trial to come to my boy away out there alone with his trouble. I had much ado not to hate that girl to whom you had given your love, and not to fancy her a most disagreeable creature with airs, and no sense, not to recognize the man in my son, and not to know his beautiful soul and the worth of his love. But then I thought perhaps he couldn't help it, poor child, that she didn't know enough to appreciate you; and likely it was God's good leading that kept you from her. But I have kept hoping that some time He would bring you to love another who was more worthy than she could have been.

"Dear, you have never said anything more about that girl, and I hope you have forgotten her, though sometimes when you were at home I noticed that deep, far-away look in your eyes, and a sadness about your lips that made me tremble lest her memory was just as bright as ever. I have wanted you to know the sweet girl Hazel Radcliffe who has been my dear friend and almost daughter—for no daughter could have been dearer than she has been to me, and I believe she loves me too as I love her. If you had been nearer I would have tried to bring you two together, at least for once, that you might judge for yourselves; but I found out that she was shy as a bird about meeting any one—though she has hosts of young men friends in her New York home—and that she would have run away if you had come. Besides, I could not have given you any reason but the truth for sending for you, and I knew God would bring you two together if it was His will. But I could not go happy from this earth without doing something towards helping you just to see her once, and so I have asked her to give you this letter with her own hand, if possible, and she has promised to do so. You will come home when I am gone and she will have to see you, and when you look on her sweet face if you do not feel as your mother does about her, it is all right, dear son; only I wanted you just to see her once because I love her so much, and because I love you. If you could forget the other and love this one it seems as though I should be glad even in heaven, but if you do not feel that way when you see her, John, don't mind my writing this letter, for it pleased me much to play this trick upon you before I left; and the dear girl must never know—unless indeed you love her—and then I do not care—for I know she will forgive me for writing this silly letter, and love me just the same.

"Dear boy, just as we never liked to say good-bye when

you went away to college, but only 'Au revoir,' so there won't be any good-bye now, only I love you.

"YOUR MOTHER."

Hazel was weeping softly when they finished the letter, and there were tears in the eyes of the son, though they were glorified by the smile that shone upon the girl as he folded the letter and said:

"Wasn't that a mother for a fellow to have? And could I do anything else than give myself when she gave all she had? And to think she picked out the very one for me that I loved of all the world, and sent her out to me because I was too set in my way to come back after her. It is just as if my mother sent you down as a gift from heaven to me, dear!" and their lips met once more in deep love and understanding.

The sun was almost setting now, and suddenly the two became aware that night was coming on. The Indian would be returning and they must plan what to do.

Brownleigh rose and went to the door to see if the Indian were in sight. He was thinking hard and fast. Then he came back and stood before the girl.

"Dear!" he said, and the tone of his voice brought the quick colour to her cheeks; it was so wonderful, so disconcerting to be looked at and spoken to in that way. She caught her breath and wondered if it were not a dream after all. "Dear," another of those deep, searching looks, "this is a big, primitive country and we do things in a most summary way out here sometimes. You must tell me if I go too fast; but could—*would* you—do you think you love me enough to marry me at once—to-night?"

"Oh!" she breathed, lifting her happy eyes. "It would be beautiful to never have to leave you again—but—you hardly know me. I am not fitted, you know. You are a great, wonderful missionary, and I—I am only a foolish girl who has fallen in love with you and can't ever be happy again without you."

She buried her face in the arm of the chair and cried happy, shamed tears, and he gathered her up in his arms and comforted her, his face shining with a glorified expression.

"Dear," he said when he could speak again, "dear, don't you know that is all I want? And don't ever talk that way again about me. I am no saint, as you'll very well find out, but I'll promise to love and cherish you as long as we both shall live. Will you marry me to-night?''

There was a silence in the little room broken only by the low crackling of the dying fire.

She lifted shy glad eyes to his, and then came and laid her two hands in his.

"If you are quite sure you want me," she breathed softly.

The rapture of his face and the tenderness of his arms assured her on that point.

"There is just one great regret I have," said the young man, lifting his eyes towards his mother's picture. "If she only could have known it was you that I loved. Why didn't I tell her your name? But then——Why, my dear, I didn't know your name. Do you realize that? I haven't known your name until now."

"I certainly did realize it," said Hazel with rosy cheeks. "It used to hurt dreadfully sometimes to think that even if you wanted to find me you wouldn't know how to go about it."

"You dear! Did you care so much?" His voice was deep and tender and his eyes were upon her.

"So much!" she breathed softly.

But the splash of red light on the floor at their feet warned them of the lateness of the hour and they turned to the immediate business of the moment.

"It is wonderful that things are just as they are to-night," said Brownleigh in his full, joyous tones. "It certainly seems providential. Bishop Vail, my father's old college chum, has been travelling through the West on missionary work for his church, and he is now at the stopping place where you spent last night. He leaves on the midnight train to-night, but we can get there long before that time, and he will marry us. There is no one I would rather have had, though the choice should have been yours. Are you going to mind very much being married in this brief and primitive manner?''

"If I minded those things I should not be worthy of your love," said Hazel softly. "No, I don't mind in the least. Only I've really nothing along to get married in—nothing suitable for a wedding gown. You won't be able to remember

146

me in bridal attire—and there won't be even Amelia Ellen for bridesmaid.'' She smiled at him mischievously.

"You darling!" he said laying his lips upon hers again. "You need no bridal attire to make you the sweetest bride that ever came to Arizona, and I shall always remember you as you are now, as the most beautiful sight my eyes ever saw. If there was time to get word to some of my colleagues off at their stations we should have a wedding reception that would outrival your New York affairs so far as enthusiasm and genuine hearty good will is concerned, but they are all from forty to a hundred miles away from here and it will be impossible. Are you sure you are not too tired to ride back to the stopping place to-night?" He looked at her anxiously. "We will hitch Billy to the wagon, and the seat has good springs. I will put in plenty of cushions and you can rest on the way, and we will not attempt to come back to-night. It would be too much for you.''

She began to protest but he went on:

"No, dear, I don't mean we'll stay in that little hole where you spent last night. That would be awful! But what would you say to camping in the same spot where we had our last talk? I have been there many times since and often spend the night there because of its sweet association with you. It is not far, you know, from the railroad—a matter of a few minutes' ride—and there is good water. We can carry my little tent and trappings, and then take as much of a wedding trip afterwards as you feel you have strength for before we return, though we shall have the rest of our lives to make one dear long wedding trip of, I hope. Will that plan suit you?''

"Oh, it will be beautiful," said Hazel with shining eyes.

"Very well, then. I will get everything ready for our start and you must rest until I call you." With that he stooped and before she realized what he was doing gently lifted her from her feet and laid her down upon his couch over in the corner, spreading a many-coloured Indian blanket over her. Then he deftly stirred up the fire, filled up the kettle, swung it back over the blaze, and with a smile went out to prepare Billy and the wagon.

Hazel lay there looking about her new home with happy eyes, noting each little touch of refinement and beauty that showed the character of the man who had lived his life alone

147

there for three long years, and wondering if it were really herself, the lonely little struggling nurse with the bitter ache in her heart, who was feeling so happy here to-day—Hazel Radcliffe, the former New York society girl, rejoicing ecstatically because she was going to marry a poor home missionary and live in a shanty! How her friends would laugh and sneer, and how Aunt Maria would lift her hands in horror and say the family was disgraced! But it did not matter about Aunt Maria. Poor Aunt Maria! She had never approved of anything that Hazel wanted to do all her life. As for her brother—and here her face took on a shade of sadness—her brother was of another world than hers and always had been. People said he was like his dead mother. Perhaps the grand man of the desert could help her brother to better things. Perhaps he would come out here to visit them and catch a vision of another kind of life and take a longing for it as she had done. He could not fail at least to see the greatness of the man she had chosen.

There was great comfort to her in this hour to remember that her father had been interested in her missionary, and had expressed a hope that she might meet him again some day. She thought her father would have been pleased at the choice she had made, for he had surely seen the vision of what was really worth while in life before he died.

Suddenly her eyes turned to the little square table over by the cupboard. What if she should set it?

She sprang up and suited the action to the thought.

Almost as a child might handle her first pewter set Hazel took the dishes from the shelves and arranged them on the table. They were pretty china dishes, with a fine old sprigged pattern of delicate flowers. She recognized them as belonging to his mother's set, and handled them reverently. It almost seemed as if that mother's presence was with her in the room as she prepared the table for her first meal with the beloved son.

She found a large white towel in the cupboard drawer that she spread on the rough little table, and set the delicate dishes upon it: two plates, two cups and saucers, knives and forks—two of everything! How it thrilled her to think that in a little while she would belong here in this dear house, a part of it, and that they two would have a right to sit together at this